GUNS OF SPRING

It took Rush Vining a whole fall and winter to see Zack Henley for what he was. They had teamed up together and fought Apaches in Arizona. Had some laughs trailing beef to Kansas. And when Zack got the foreman's job at Charlie Magee's Tres Pinos, it was no deal without Rush as segundo . . . Then Magee somehow died, and, come spring, Rush found himself staring up the barrel of his best buddy's gun!

DEAN OWEN

GUNS
OF SPRING

Complete and Unabridged

LINFORD
Leicester

First Linford Edition
published December 1989

British Library CIP Data

Owen, Dean
    Guns of spring.—Large print ed.—
Linford western library
I. Title
813'.54[F]

ISBN 0-7089-6771-X

Published by
F. A. Thorpe (Publishing) Ltd.
Anstey, Leicestershire

Set by Rowland Phototypesetting Ltd.
Bury St. Edmunds, Suffolk
Printed and bound in Great Britain by
T. J. Press (Padstow) Ltd., Padstow, Cornwall

1

ABOVE the howling wind that slashed at the big Tres Pinos wagon, Rush Vining heard his employer shout, "By God, there's my boy now. And he's brung a woman with him!" The last held a note of disappointment.

Rush's strong arms hauled in on the lines as he swung the team to a loading platform in front of the Taylor Store. At his side on the high seat Charlie Magee, wizened, his furry face projecting from the high collar of a sheepskin jacket, gestured at a lean young man standing with a girl on the walk.

"Lee, it's me, your poppa!" Charlie Magee yelled down from the wagon.

His son Lee lifted a gloved hand. "Took you long enough to get here!"

Rush set the brake on the big wagon and shot a blue-eyed glance at the old man's heir, noting the rather elegant gentleman's black coat. Then he was busy quieting the team. Behind the wagon two men dismounted; the Tres Pinos escort. They stood beside their horses in the wind, beating gloved hands together against the cold. They stared at Lee Magee and the girl, as if resenting the fact that they had been forced to make a long ride just to meet these passengers from the Del Norte stage.

Charlie Magee climbed stiffly down from the wagon to pump the hand of his son and look up into the younger, sullenly handsome face as if to measure his height.

"You ain't much taller," Charlie Magee observed in his thin old voice, "than you was when you left here at fifteen."

"Some bigger, Poppa, in eight years. . . . It's been a miserable wait for us."

"Wheeler, Texas, ain't much of a bright spot, I agree." The old man looked at the girl. "Who's she?"

"My wife. Poppa, the stage got in day

2

before yesterday. I thought surely you'd be here—"

"Your *wife!*"

Rush saw the girl lick her lips; her intense blue eyes in a pale but pretty face reflected surprise and a shred of fear at the old man's vehemence. Rush couldn't tell much about her figure because she was buttoned to her throat in a heavy gray traveling cloak. Screaming wind threatened to rip a rather ridiculous hat from her golden head.

"This is Eloise, Poppa," Lee Magee introduced his wife.

The girl murmured something Rush could not hear. He tied the team, reflecting that Lee Magee had picked himself a young one.

Lee nodded at Rush. "Who's he, Poppa?"

"Rush Vining. Been with me two years. My segundo. Him and Zack Henley signed on at the same time. Zack's my foreman. You'll meet him at the ranch."

Charlie Magee introduced them, but Lee only gave a brief jerk of his head and did not offer to remove a glove in order to shake hands. Behind the wagon, out of the wind, stood the two Tres Pinos hands, Bagley and Tinker, armed with rifle and belt gun. Charlie Magee did not bother to introduce them to Lee.

As Charlie had a few words with his son, a bulky man with a badge pinned to his coat stepped from a saloon next door. At sight of the rancher, he quickened his pace. "Charlie, you old son of a—" Upon seeing the girl, he broke off. He slapped the old cattleman on the arm. "I heard your boy was waitin' here for you. Fine lookin' fella, ain't he, Charlie." He turned to look at the girl, who was biting her lips at the cold. "Pretty wife."

"She's kind of lean in the shank from what I can see," Charlie grunted. "Chores'll put some meat on her."

Lee Magee had overheard the remark. "Poppa, she's not going to do chores. Let's get that straight right now."

Rush wondered how the old man would take such defiance. Instead of bristling, he seemed to shrink. A white-bearded doll

4

beside his tall son, more embarrassed than angry. He covered it by introducing the man with the badge as Sheriff Tom Faulkner.

"A good man to know, Lee."

Lee gave the sheriff a nod, then said, "Poppa, let's get home. I'm sick of this town."

Eloise, at his side, slapped at long skirts to keep them from being windblown. She stared in a kind of frightened fascination at the two Tres Pinos hands behind the wagon, at the big six-shooters, the rifles. And Rush had to admit they probably did look formidable to the girl. He shared her obvious aversion to the pair; he didn't like them either.

The sheriff, turning from an appreciative glance at two inches of the girl's ankle that the wind had thoughtfully exposed, said, "Charlie, everything all right down your way?"

Charlie Magee pulled his troubled gaze from the son he had not seen for so long. "Be glad when this goddam winter is done," he told the sheriff.

5

"S'pose you notice I took your advice. Appointed Jim Boomer deputy. Hope he's doin' a job for you, Charlie."

"Jim's fat in the butt and thin in the brain. But he's the kind of deputy I favor. Don't horn in where he ain't wanted."

The sheriff then looked over at Rush beside the wagon. Disapproval touched the lawman's wind-blown face as he stared at Rush, tall, with dark brown hair that curled about the neck of his fleece-lined jacket. A Kiowa nose of jutting bone, a generous mouth. Eyes, a lighter shade of blue than the girl's, locked with the sheriff's gaze.

Faulkner nudged Charlie Magee. "Rush here been behaving himself?"

The old man snapped, "How many times I got to tell you. I size a man up. If I figure I can trust him, I do it all the way."

"Well, I didn't mean to rile you none—"

"Rush told me all about his trouble when I hired him on. He just happened to get caught. A lot of us didn't."

6

Sheriff Faulkner changed the subject. "There's talk that some Comanche bucks busted outa the reservation. Better keep your eyes open on the way home."

This news caused Rush Vining's mouth to dry and he shot a glance at Lee's wife. What a prize the golden one would be. Only a few short years had passed since the Comanche made a business of allowing captive women to be ransomed. And the younger generation had probably not forgotten the game.

The howling wind came up again to hurl sand against the front of the store. Charlie Magee yelled at the two men who had acted as escort for the wagon. "We'll start loadin' the wagon now!" Then he turned to his son. "Lee, reckon you won't mind waiting—"

"We've waited long enough—"

"I brung the wagon to pick up supplies," Charlie explained to his son. "Figured I might as well freight home some grub along with my son." The old man tried to laugh. "I didn't plan on you havin' a woman with you."

"Get the supplies in Pilot Gap, Poppa. I'm dead tired." Then Lee added, his voice almost a whine, "And I suppose Eloise is too."

"All right. You and the wife ride in back. Lee, gimme a hand with this tailgate."

When Lee hesitated, Rush walked to the rear of the wagon and unchained the gate. Eloise Magee peered into the wagon, looking uncertain as to just how she was supposed to climb in. Rush settled it by catching her at the arms. He swung her up into the wagon. She seemed very light, almost frail. But her soft hair smelled good against his face. Like a spring day.

Then Rush and the old man borrowed blankets from the store and a buffalo robe. When Lee and his wife were settled in the wagon with the high sideboards, Rush brought out a portmanteau and two carpetbags from the hotel next door.

From the high wagon seat Rush glanced down at Lee, who was saying something to Eloise. Lee seemed annoyed. Rush noticed it was Lee who wore the buffalo robe across his shoulders instead of the girl. Rush felt ten years older than Lee, yet he knew this softly handsome son of Charlie's was only two years younger.

Bagley and Tinker had mounted up, undoubtedly relieved that they hadn't had to strain their backs at loading the wagon. Zack, the foreman, had hired on the pair a month back. And it was Zack who had insisted they ride as escort for the wagon.

Rush swung the wagon in the rutted street to head in the direction of Tres Pinos ranch to the south. Just before leaving town Rush glanced at the pair riding behind the wagon. Or supposed to be riding there. Only Bagley was near the tailgate; Tinker, lank, redhaired, spurred after the heavyset Bagley. Tinker had made a trip to the saloon. The front of his blanket coat bulged.

For a moment Rush considered making an issue out of them bringing a bottle for the return trip, then decided there were already enough problems with the girl.

Charlie Magee called down to his son,

"Never figured on you bringin' a bride home, Lee."

"Eloise and I have been married almost a year."

"When you wrote you wanted to come home at long last and learn ranchin', you could have told me you had a wife."

"Why would you be interested, Poppa? I've had only two letters in eight years."

"Lee, please don't quarrel," Rush heard the girl say.

The wagon rumbled south, with Rush scanning the brushy hills, watching for dust sign against the metallic blue of the sky. Periodically there were stories of Comanche break outs. In this country you could never gamble that it was only a rumor.

The old man said grudgingly, turning his head again, "Sorry to hear that your Aunt Lottie died." Then to Rush, "She was my wife's sister. Lee went east to live with her."

Rush glanced back at Bagley and Tinker, saw the latter stuff something back into his blanket coat. Tonight when they camped Rush intended to warn them to hold up on the drinking. Time enough for that later on. Rush turned his attention to the road that angled across the country scarred by arroyos, the flats and ridges clumped with mesquite and cholla. He wondered what changes the arrival of Charlie's son would make at Tres Pinos. Zack Henley, when he first heard the boy was coming home, hadn't liked the idea at all. Lee bringing a pretty wife might complicate all their lives. There were no women at Tres Pinos and the winters were long and men grew restive.

To the south he could see the Del Carmens humped against the sky; to his right were the Chisos and beyond them the river and Mexico. Rush reflected on the fact that he had worked at Tres Pinos for over a year before he knew that Charlie Magee even had a son.

Charlie was talking about the college Lee had gone to in New Jersey. "Rush here has had schooling," the old man said to his son. The wind had died; he no longer had to shout.

"How exceedingly interesting," Lee said caustically.

"Rush went to Pike Academy outa San Antone."

"Only for a year," Rush put in. He wanted to set it straight so Lee wouldn't think he considered Pike the equal of that school Lee had attended called Princeton.

Late in the day they made camp. Even though the wind had tapered to occasional gusts, Rush pulled the wagon against a cut bank to give them protection, in case it should howl to life during the night.

Rifle in hand, Rush swung down. Under his heavy coat he wore a holstered .44. He told Bagley and Tinker to rustle up firewood. And when they unsaddled and started to forage for wood, Rush said, "Mr. Magee, I'll camp away from the wagon. To give you and your wife some privacy." He was speaking to the old man's son.

"I expected you would," Lee said shortly and stared at the shadowy mesquite growing high as the wagon.

Lon Tinker brought in the first

armload of wood and dumped it some distance away at a ring of smoke-blackened rocks. Then he tipped back his hat on fiery red hair. In the center of his forehead a bone white scar had the shape of a crooked finger.

"Got any other chores, *boss?*" he asked in a surly voice.

Rush walked over. "Easy on the drinking," Rush warned. He gave Tinker a hard look. "Pass the word to Bagley when he comes in." Bagley was afoot, hunting wood.

Rush tramped back to the wagon. Leaning his rifle against a wheel, he began to unharness the team. It was then that he heard a horse approaching the camp at a walk.

Rush caught up his rifle. "Company coming, Mr. Magee," he said to the old man.

Charlie Magee had already snatched his Sharps from the wagon bed. His son peered white-faced out of the rear of the wagon. Without looking around, the old man removed a revolver from his belt and placed it on the tailgate.

"Lee, you take my pistol," Charlie Magee said tensely. But Lee, Rush noticed, seemed frozen, making no move toward the weapon.

Bagley had returned to camp with wood, which he dumped on the pile Tinker had already brought in. Both men were looking at a rider who appeared through the mesquite. A man with a long, dark, rather handsome face. A lean man in the saddle of a gray.

At sight of the new arrival Bagley and Tinker lowered the rifles they had been holding.

Bagley's heavy shoulders settled. "Hiya, Oro," he said to the newcomer and Tinker also grunted a greeting.

Oro Lance nodded to the pair, then rode on to the wagon. His horse threw a steamy breath into the raw afternoon. Lance stepped down, apparently fascinated at sight of the pale-haired girl in the wagon bed. As he stared, his slim, dark fingers toyed with a gold piece strung on his rawhide chin strap.

Nothing had been added to Rush's day by the appearance of Oro Lance.

"Hello, Mr. Magee," Lance said to the old man, at last tearing his yellow-flecked eyes from the girl. "Spotted your camp." He looked at Rush. "Howdy, Rush."

Charlie Magee's furry jaw was out-thrust. "You know this fella, Rush?" he snapped without turning his head.

Zack and I met him a few years back," Rush admitted. "In Monterrey."

"How's my old friend Zack these days?" Lance drawled.

Before Rush could reply, Charlie Magee lifted his Sharps. "Lance, I don't favor a man like you. Anybody who stirs up trouble in Mexico ain't no friend of mine."

Lance's thin lips tightened. "Happened a long time ago, Mr. Magee. I supplied the *revolución* with cattle—"

"Wet cattle," Charlie Magee snapped.

"Careful now," Lance warned.

"I mean it!"

Rush steadied his rifle. His gaze swung to Bagley, then to Tinker who was lighting a small fire in the ring of rocks.

Rush stepped away from the wagon, the rifle centered on Lance. "You'd better leave. Mr. Magee doesn't want you here."

Rush stiffened as Lance made a slight movement toward the tail of his black coat. Even now, with a rifle on the man, Rush had no wish to tangle with a gunhand of Lance's reputation. But damned if he'd back down.

"Move," Rush said coldly.

Lance studied Rush's face that reflected most everything the frontier could throw at a man, then let his hand fall loosely to his side.

"In town I heard there are Comanches out, Mr. Magee," Lance said to the old man. "I thought it might be neighborly to ride with you."

"The Comanche ain't been out in five years."

"You might be able to use an extra gun—"

16

"My segundo told you to clear out," Charlie interrupted.

Lance seemed to take the affront with a minimum of anger. Shrugging his black-clad shoulders, he mounted. "Sorry you feel this way, Magee."

Turning his horse, he gave Bagley and Tinker a nod, then rode back through the mesquite. Rush climbed to the lip of the cut bank to watch Lance head back in the direction of Wheeler. Only when the man was a black dot against the encroaching twilight did Rush return to camp.

Charlie Magee was glaring at his son. "Why didn't you pick up the pistol like I told you?"

"You and your segundo seemed to be handling the situation," was Lee's nervous reply.

"You better learn to act quick. One day you just might have to defend your wife."

Lee Magee turned red. "If and when, I'll defend her."

When Rush finished unharnessing the team he walked over to Tinker who was

17

stirring coffee in a pot taken from a box in the wagon. Bagley dropped more wood on the fire.

"How well do you know Oro Lance?" Rush demanded.

"Seen him in town is all," the black-haired Bagley said.

"He buys drinks at O'Hale's," put in Tinker. "Ain't no law against me an' Clyde drinkin' his whisky."

Rush stared into Tinker's pale gray eyes. "As long as you work for Tres Pinos," Rush said—and that might not be very long, he wanted to add— "stay away from Lance."

The evening meal was eaten in silence around the fire in the growing darkness; bacon and cold biscuits brought from the ranch. Coffee was scalding.

When Lee and his wife retired Rush helped the old man spread blankets beneath the wagon. When he had finished he found Eloise peering down at him over the tailgate. In the wash of firelight he could see her pale face, almost peaked, her long yellow hair that she no longer tried to keep pinned.

"Mr. Vining, is it true about the—Indians?" She sounded frightened. "I mean there being trouble?"

"Don't worry about it." Rush smiled. "Nothing will happen."

"Everything is so strange—so terrifying." She looked toward the fire where Tinker and Bagley were two blobs of shadow.

Lee took his wife's place at the tailgate. "You weren't very civil to that man Lance," he said to Rush. "I don't think it would have hurt to let him eat with us."

"Rush figured I didn't want him around," the old man snapped, coming up in the darkness. "I don't like gunslicks."

"You haven't changed, Poppa. You antagonize everyone."

Rush got his own blankets and placed them a dozen yards from the dying fire. In the brush *animales* made small sounds in the winter night.

The old man came over. "Rush, you figure I talked too tough to Oro Lance?"

Rush said, "I thought he was still in Mexico," without answering the question.

"What you think of them two?" Charlie pointed at the cowhands lounging by the coals.

Rush chose his words. He didn't want to put his friend Zack in a bad light. "Zack hired them on to run the horse camp. I haven't been down that way lately, so I haven't had much to do with them."

"I don't like 'em worth a damn," said the old man. "But I got to admit I ain't paid much attention to what's been goin' on. Been kind of fogged up in my mind ever since Lee wrote that he was comin' home." Then Charlie Magee's voice broke as he added, "Sometimes I wonder why the hell he even bothered."

"Likely he'll adjust to the country," Rush said.

"One thing, he's got a puny wife. A man needs a woman with some heft to her—"

"I think Lee's wife has spunk. It'll show up once she gets used to things here."

"Mebby I been too hard on Lee. His momma died when he was born. And I guess I—I almost hated the kid." Charlie stood with his white head bowed. "I s'pose it's time I made it up—" The old man's voice trailed away and in the early darkness Rush had the uncomfortable feeling that Charlie Magee, tough as a Texas boot, was wiping tears from his bearded face.

In Pilot Gap there were those who said that when he died—which he was probably too ornery to do—there wouldn't be enough tears shed to water a sotol spear. Those in town didn't really know Charlie Magee. To them he was just an old hellion who taunted local merchants by shipping in supplies from Wheeler where he could sometimes save a dollar a barrel on flour. Or buy his whisky from across the river. They didn't realize that he was a lonely old man, even though he had more cows than he could brand, more sections of land than he could cross in three days of riding. He had fought drought and suffered through the years when a hide was worth ten times the meat on a longhorn's bones. In his earlier days he had battled beside Sam Houston and come home to find his ranch buildings leveled by the Comanche. At an age when most men welcomed the first of their grandchildren, he had taken a wife and moved farther west.

"Been mulling things over in my mind lately, Rush," Charlie Magee said, his voice now under control. "My boy comin' home changes things. Bringin' a wife changes it even more. We'll talk about it come mornin' . . . reckon it's up to you an' me to stand guard tonight."

"I'll take first watch," Rush said.

He waited until the old man had rolled up his blankets under the wagon. Then Rush, rifle in hand, walked over to where Bagley and Tinker squatted by the coals, talking in low tones. They broke off and looked around at him. Mingled with the stink of greasewood was a strong odor of alcohol.

Rush sank to his bootheels. "Zack hired you," he said quietly. "And Zack's my friend. But if one head of Tres Pinos beef turns up missing I'll start looking close to home."

"Why'd you say a thing like that?" Bagley demanded.

"The fact that you're on speaking terms with Oro Lance."

"You ain't the boss, Zack is," Tinker cut in coldly. Sparks broke from the bed of coals and drifted toward the starry sky.

Rush pointed with his rifle barrel at something Tinker held against his thigh, away from Rush.

"Let's see what you've got there," Rush said.

Tinker hesitated, then picked up a bottle. Rush snatched it from his hand, worked the cork loose with his teeth, then emptied it on the ground.

"You got nerve doin' that," Tinker snarled. "You damn jailbird!"

"Don't say that again," Rush warned quietly. And for a moment he wondered if they had enough Texas whisky in their bloodstream to spur them into some dangerous and irrational act.

Rush kicked the empty bottle into the brush. "Don't you boys give us any trouble. Understand?"

Then he backed to his blankets. Sinking to his bed, he vowed that upon his return to Tres Pinos, he would insist that Zack fire them. For three months or so, ever since Zack learned that Lee Magee was coming home, the big foreman had been making some odd moves. At least to Rush's way of thinking. Zack would complain about the men. And one by one the old hands were replaced. Charlie Magee had admitted tonight that he had been so upset over his son's return to Texas that there had been room for little else in his mind.

Several times Rush had tried to argue with Zack against the firing of the old hands, even making a halfway joke out of it so as not to give Zack the idea he was being pressured. Zack was too dangerous a man, all two hundred and forty-five pounds of him, for even a friend like Rush to push around. And as segundo, Rush was in no position to complain directly to Charlie Magee about the way Zack seemed to be handling things lately. To Zack the old man was "Charlie." To Rush and the rest of the crew he was "Mr. Magee."

It was one thing the old man was firm on, even though he had lately taken to asking Rush to ride with him across Tres Pino range. Then the old man would unburden himself about his dead wife and his son. Rush would listen, rarely commenting.

"Ain't made any friends in my lifetime," the old man said one day. "Too cussed, I reckon. Now take you an' Zack. You're close as two rattles in a sidewinder's tail. You're loyal, Rush. It's one thing I admire about you."

Rush waited till long past midnight before awakening the old man to his turn of guard duty. It was on the tip of

Rush's tongue to mention that it wouldn't hurt Lee to crawl out of his warm blankets and take his father's trick. But he didn't.

2

IN the morning Rush had to break a sheet of creek ice with his boot heel so that the horses could drink. Tinker and Bagley, Rush observed, were slow in getting out of their blankets. Bagley stood up, scratching himself. He staggered. Rush knew then that he should have hunted for a second bottle.

Because Charlie Magee was in a hurry to get home, they ate cold bacon left over from the night before and more of the tough cookhouse biscuits. Eloise did not eat. In the wan morning light she seemed most frail, the fear still lurking in her large blue eyes. Occasionally Rush would find her looking at him. He had the uncomfortable feeling that she disliked him. He wondered if she could have over-heard Tinker's snarl, "Jailbird!"

And of course in town Sheriff Faulkner had had to go and prove how short and unrelenting his memory was by asking, "Rush been behaving himself?"

Rush jerked his head at Tinker and Bagley. He told them to harness the wagon team.

"Give 'em a hand, Lee," Charlie Magee snapped at his son. "Time you learned."

"Poppa, I don't know one thing about horses and harness."

"You're twenty-three, boy," the old man said. "If you aim to take over Tres Pinos, you better learn all you can."

A sour smile almost spoiled Lee's good looks. "You'll likely live forever."

"No," said Charlie, bracing his thin bowed legs. "I was fifty-one years old when you was born. You better think about it, boy. There ain't nobody else on this God's earth to take over but you." The old man reached out to place a hand on Rush's arm. "You an' Rush Vining here. And my foreman Zack."

Surprised, Rush looked down at the furry old face.

Lee stared in growing anger. "Poppa, you mean your foreman. And your segundo. Share Tres Pinos with me? Is that what you're trying to say?"

"You each get fiften per cent—"

Eloise broke in. "But he's your own *son!*" Her full red mouth held a pressure whiteness at the corners. She was a scrawny one, Rush decided.

"While I live, I keep fifty-five per cent of Tres Pinos," Charlie Magee said. "We'll call it the Tres Pinos Cattle Company. When I go, then Lee gets my share, plus his own."

Lee Magee turned on Rush. "I suppose you used your Pike Academy charm to talk my father into this!" he accused.

Rush had recovered from his initial surprise. He fought down an urge to lift Lee from the ground and shake the Tres Pinos heir until his boots knocked together.

"It's the first I knew about it, Mr. Magee," he told Lee.

Charlie Magee said, "Papers was fixed up with Joe Flannery. He's my lawyer. I kept it as a surprise. And Rush, from here on out we use first names. The three of us. You understand, Lee?"

Lee's face was flushed. Tinker and Bagley looked on as they finished with the last of harness buckles and straps.

"Good thing I came back from Texas when I did." Lee's voice shook. "Another year and my father would have given away the whole ranch!"

Charlie glared at his son. "I'm still big enough to take a rope end to your butt."

"That I doubt. And please watch how you talk in front of my wife. Some of your language—"

"Let's get rollin'," Charlie Magee snapped.

"Sure, Mr. Magee," Rush said. And when the old man, one booted foot on a wheel hub, looked at him, Rush changed it to, "Sure, Charlie."

"That's better." A faint smile flickered across the bearded lips.

Lee attempted to swing his wife into the wagon bed as Rush had done. But he lost his balance. Eloise stumbled, her skirts flying.

Clyde Bagley, observing this, said to Tinker, "Now yonderly is a prime filly to take to bed. If her husband don't know what to do with her, by God I do."

His laughter slid off into a hoarse sound of surprise, not realizing till then that Rush had been directly behind him. Rush spun him around.

For an instant Bagley seemed startled at the rage on Rush's face. Then his heavy shoulders stiffened. He jammed a hand toward his revolver. Before the move could be completed Rush lashed out, every ounce of his hundred and eighty pounds, the leverage of shoulder and leg, going into the blow. So savage and sudden was the attack that Bagley was able to make only one futile attempt to block the blow with his left forearm. Rush's fist brushed it aside to land squarely on the jaw. Upward the fist drove, knuckles twisting clear to the eye and beyond.

Tinker, startled, leaped aside as Bagley was smashed back against the wagon. There Bagley seemed to hang for an instant. Then he collapsed, face down in the thick Texas dust. Immediately he began to make hoarse choking sounds.

Rush stood, revolver in hand, the barrel slanted at Tinker. But the raw-boned redhead made no move to grab his own gun, but stared in disbelief at Bagley gasping on the ground.

In the stunned silence, with Charlie Magee peering down from the high wagon seat, Eloise Magee rushed up. Her face was stricken as she tugged at one of Bagley's heavy arms.

"He'll smother in dust!" she cried, "Help me!"

Rush bent to give her a hand, but she flashed him a glance of scorn. "Not *you!*"

It was Lee who finally turned Bagley over on his back. Bagley's breathing became less ragged. The side of his face bled into the dust.

Slowly Eloise straightened, a loathing in her eyes. "What a brutal, inhuman thing to do!" she said to Rush. "Never have I seen anything so vicious!"

Rush knew he had to make a stand with Tinker and Bagley. "Tinker, any money you two have coming will be left at O'Hale's Saloon. Along with your weapons. Now get Bagley out of here!"

It was ten minutes before Bagley revived sufficiently to sit a saddle.

Tinker said, "Ain't right to send a man out with no gun!"

"This time it's right," Rush snapped.

And Tinker seemed so impressed by the way Rush had handled things that he ceased to argue. He rode out with Bagley, the latter swaying in the saddle, one eye completely closed.

Rush looked around at the old man, wondering if he would have something to say about the segundo doing the firing. Charlie said nothing.

As Rush was ready to chain up the tailgate, Eloise came to him, "Mr. Vining, I understand from my father-in-law that Bagley made an insulting remark. I apologize for what I said to you."

Lee Magee's face was flushed as he leveled a finger at Rush. "Vining, when my wife's honor needs defending, I'll be the one to do it!"

"Rush is a partner now," Charlie Magee cut in coldly from the wagon seat. "You better remember that, Lee. And get along with him."

By mid-afternoon they came within sight of Tres Pinos headquarters; for hours now they had passed Tres Pinos cattle, branded with three pines.

"Yonderly is your new home, daughter." Charlie Magee pointed a bony finger at the buildings.

Eloise peered silently over the wagon sideboard into the weak winter sun. "It's quite nice." She sounded depressed.

Rush was glad for his own glimpse of the barn, the circular stone corrals, the big bunkhouse with the lean-to on one end where he and Zack had their quarters. Beyond, across the wide yard, surrounded by gaunt and leafless cottonwoods, was the sprawling main house with its mud walls and roof, fronted by a sagging veranda. As he drove the wagon toward the big house, Rush saw Zack Henley in front of a corral. Rush lifted a hand.

Zack, looming wide as a house door, was talking to Vic Peden, the sinewy little horsebreaker. Peden was the last of the old hands that Zack had not replaced over a period of months. A good horsebreaker was not easy to find.

Zack swung into the saddle of a sorrel and came pounding up to where Rush had halted the wagon in front of the house.

"Was kind of worried," Zack boomed, swinging down from the big horse that was sturdy enough to pack his weight. "Heard that Comanches was out between here and Wheeler."

Rush heard Eloise give a frightened sound under her breath as Lee helped her from the wagon. Mention of Indian trouble seemed to upset her.

Zack stood eyeing her, large hands on hips, hat shoved back on wiry dark hair. Zack's slate-gray eyes in the broad face seemed pleased by what he saw. Rush wanted to deepen Zack's pleasure by telling him about the fifteen per cent they each now owned in the ranch. Zack was always waiting for their luck to turn. It had and quickly.

Charlie Magee was introducing his daughter-in-law and son to Zack.

Zack beamed on Eloise, swept off his hat and gave a deep bow, shaggy hair falling across his face. "Perfectly charmed, ma'am, to make your acquaintance." Then he put on his hat and shot out a big hand at Lee. "This sure is a *genu-wyne* pleasure, Lee. Your poppa has talked about you so much I feel you an' me are already friends."

Lee shook hands, apparently impressed by Zack's size and the fact that the big revolver he wore had the nude figure of a woman carved into the ivory grip.

Charlie Magee said, "Zack, you and Rush come to the house for supper. Reckon Lee's wife will fix us a meal."

Eloise's mouth fell open. "I—I can't cook."

And as the old man stared in disbelief, Lee said stiffly, "Poppa, I plan to get a woman to do the house chores and the cooking. Eloise will have an easier time of it than my poor mother."

Charlie bristled. Rush expected an explosion, but the old man seemed to run out of steam. "Reckon we'll all eat together at the cookshack—"

"I'd rather Eloise didn't associate with the men." Lee suggested that trays of hot food could be sent up from the cookshack.

When Lee and the girl entered the house, with its thick walls, the narrow windows, it seemed to Rush that Charlie Magee had suddenly shriveled. That he had aged.

Rush hoped to get the old man's mind off his son by changing the subject. "Zack, I've got good news." He told Zack about the partnership. "Charlie's been generous to us."

The old man was still staring at the house where his son had disappeared. "Been planning the partnership for some time," he grunted. "So I done it."

"Well, well," Zack said indifferently.

When the old man had shuffled into the house, Rush said, "Zack, you don't seem elated about the partnership."

"Fifteen per cent ain't bigger than a fly speck on a mule's ass."

"I consider myself lucky."

"And since when do *you* call him Charlie?" Then Zack smiled to take the sting out of it. "For a segundo, you ride a pretty tall saddle."

They walked toward their quarters, as one of the hands drove the wagon to the barn.

"So the old man's son has come home at long last," Zack mused. "Lee Magee. Lah—de—dah." Zack laughed.

"He'll toughen up."

Zack glanced at Rush's right hand. "How'd you skin your knuckles? Did you bust Sheriff Faulkner in the mouth? For cussin' you out as usual 'cause you once shot up his shirttail kin?"

"A period in my life I'd rather forget." Some of the hands were in the cookshack doorway, awaiting the call to supper. None of them greeted Rush. Only Vic

38

Peden, who was washing up outside, asked how things were in Wheeler. Rush told the little horsebreaker that the wind had come straight out of Canada.

Zack led the way into their quarters. "That's quite a filly Lee brung home. Makes a man itch just to look at her."

"I think she's scared half to death of Texas," Rush said.

Zack's thick lips smiled. "Some quiet night I just might unscare her." Zack chuckled deep in his large chest.

3

RUSH sailed his hat to an antler rack, not liking the remark. He turned to study Zack's strong profile, the nose flattened in some forgotten brawl, the thick neck, the spread of powerful shoulders.

"I hit Bagley, not Sheriff Faulkner," Rush said, deciding to settle the issue.

"I know. They come ridin' in a few hours back," Zack said with a hard grin. "They could travel faster than you could with the wagon. Clyde's face looks like it got caught under a stampede."

"I fired them."

Zack chewed on a splinter of wood. "I hire and fire. Not you!"

Rush related the remark Bagley had made about Lee's wife. "She's going to have a rough enough time as it is without the men bothering her."

"If Lee ain't got guts enough to stand

up for his own wife, she deserves anything said about her."

"Don't push this, Zack," Rush warned.

Zack laughed and plopped himself down on his bunk across the room. "You caught me in a good humor. Lucky for you, Rush."

Rush sank to his own bunk. His arms were tired from handling the team. Much better to have taken saddlers, but the old man didn't ride much these days because of an ache in his hip. Last fall he had tripped over a shovel someone had left near the barn wall. Just as well they had taken the wagon though, Rush reflected; would have been a hard saddle trip for Eloise. She didn't look like much of a rider, and she had been afraid of the wagon team every time she passed near them.

Rush looked around, feeling a new strangeness in these quarters he shared with Zack. Lately Zack had lost a lot of his good humor. Rush had felt an increasing pressure to maintain a reasonable relationship with his friend and foreman.

He liked this room with its Indian rugs on the floor, the rifle racks on the wall. For two years it had been his home. At one end of the room was an oak table that was supposed to be Zack's desk. But Rush sat there more often, keeping the books straight. He started to unbuckle his gunbelt, then reconsidered. It was the first time he had hesitated to remove his gun in Zack's presence.

Zack had removed his boots and now rubbed at large toes. "Never really figured Lee would come home."

"It's where he belongs," Rush said.

"Now Lee will stumble onto all that luck you and me been huntin' all these years."

"Lee was just smart enough to pick the right father."

"You can joke about it. You're still near a kid, Rush. When a man's thirty-four like me he starts frettin' about the sand that runs outa his hour glass."

"That's almost poetic." Rush grinned to try and lighten the mood.

"When a man's my age, he grabs his luck. He hangs onto it."

Something in the way Zack looked at him put a faint chill at the back of Rush's neck. He needed a shave and a drink and some decent food.

"I think we're pretty lucky as it is, Zack."

"What's fifteen per cent of four thousand head of beef? Not a hell of a lot, Rush."

"Charlie dealt us a good hand of poker," Rush reminded quietly. "Let's not make him sorry."

"Rush, you're a damn funny cuss."

"Most of us are, one way or another." Zack leaned forward on the bunk, thick forearms crossed on his knees. "When we teamed up we was flat busted. But that first night we was together I won thirty dollars at monte."

"And I found a gold piece in the alley behind the Gadsen Saloon," Rush put in.

"We both figured it was a good sign.

That you and me would have luck together."

"We've done pretty well since that night in Santa Fe."

"We tried to find that luck in Arizona," Zack continued. "But the 'Paches was thicker than flies around a hog butcher. We tried it in Monterrey. But the greasers was too busy killin' each other off in a revolution. Then we trailed beef to Kansas."

"And gained a rep for having few trail losses."

Zack rubbed dirt from between his toes. "When Charlie Magee's foreman got a cow horn through his gut, I was sent for."

"And you insisted that if you were hired on, Charlie Magee also had to take me. Or it was no deal."

Zack sat back on the bunk, rope supports groaning from his weight. "Well, I see you remember. I thought that the way you and the old man been ridin' around with your heads together

44

lately that you wouldn't remember about old Zack."

"Listen, our friendship has meant a lot to me." Rush hesitated, grinding his hands together at a bitter memory. "When I got out of jail that time I was bitter. I could have gone the wrong way. I've always felt that meeting up with you helped me—"

"What you and the old man been talkin' about on them rides, anyhow?"

"About his son mostly. Sorry that he practically hated the boy when he was growing up here. Blamed his wife for dying on him and took it out on the boy. Charlie wanted Lee to come home. And yet at the same time he dreaded the idea."

"Charlie never talks to me about anything but cows."

Rush tried to smile. "He figures you're a working foreman. I'm the lazy one who always has time to listen."

For a moment Zack's gray eyes were cold as mountain ice. Then his mouth quirked at one corner. "With all your book learnin' you never got what I got.

Once I make up my mind to somethin',
I never stop. I'm tough, Rush."

"I've also acquired a certain toughness."

"Not my kind. My kind you don't
learn out of no book."

Rush stood up as somebody began to
pound on the iron bar outside the cookshack; the call to supper.

"Let's go see what the cook can fry up
for us," Rush suggested.

Zack stomped into his boots, then
draped a heavy arm across Rush's
shoulders. "We've rode a good ways
together in five years," Zack said with
false heartiness. "It's the longest we ever
stayed on a job."

"We've been drifters. But not now. We
have a reason for sticking."

"You let ol' Zack figure out which fork
in the trail it's best for us to take."

Rush stepped out from under Zack's
arm. "We'd better settle something,
Zack. What about Tinker and Bagley?"

"Why, they're at their old jobs. At the

hoss camp." Zack leaned forward. "Rush, just let it drop, huh."

"What's so important about that pair?"

"Roundup ain't far off. We need good hands. They're two of the best."

"And they also know Oro Lance." Rush watched Zack's face. "Lance came to our camp. Rather conveniently, I thought."

"Ain't nothin' wrong in being neighborly."

"That's the way Lance put it. I had a feeling something was up. But I couldn't decide what it was. Unless Lance thought he could get on the good side of the old man in some way—"

Zack took a hitch at his wide gunbelt. "Oro's all right. You remember that, Rush. He knows his way around the greasers across the river." Zack stabbed him with a steel-gray eye. "That just might come in handy for you and me, Rush."

"Lance is no man to fool with—"

"I fooled with him once," Zack reminded with a grin. He touched the

47

ivory-butted gun at his belt. "Remember the night I won this off him? He was playin' poor poker that time."

"The Mexicans were looking for him with a hang-rope. Hardly the time for a man to keep his mind on cards."

"Oro just happened to pick the wrong side in the *revolución*."

"Charlie Magee doesn't like him. That also goes for Bagley and Tinker."

"I'm runnin' things here, Rush. Mebby you haven't noticed, but the old man is poorly. Can't ride much. But he still squeezes a dollar till his hand bleeds."

"He's been damned good to us, Zack. Being a partner in a ranch this size is my kind of luck. I don't want to see it ruined."

"Yeah, for a jailbird, you're doin' pretty good," Zack joshed.

"Tinker called me that yesterday. I warned him not to say it again." Rush's voice was flat. "I don't want to hear it from you either."

"Hell, I was only funnin'."

"Kick Tinker and his friend off the

place. And don't get yourself tied in with Oro Lance."

"That's the quickest way to get me to do somethin'. Tell me I *can't!*" Their eyes locked for a long moment in the big dusty room, then Zack's mouth relaxed. He knuckled Rush on the arm. "Come on, let's go get us a slab of that fried Tres Pinos beef. That we own thirty per cent of between us." Zack gave a hearty laugh.

4

THE next day Charlie Magee got a Mexican woman named Consuelo to come out from the settlement in Pilot Gap to do the cooking and keep house for Eloise. Several times that week Rush tried again to bring up the subject of firing the pair at the horse camp, but Zack ignored him.

Rush rarely saw the old man these days. Once he tried to get his ear, but Charlie Magee seemed preoccupied with problems that involved his son and daughter-in-law. If the old man cared that Bagley and Tinker were running the horse camp he gave no sign. It was too far for him to ride these days, clear down to Oatman Springs. Town was as far as he ever rode.

And Rush's duties hadn't taken him as far south as the camp. He hadn't seen the pair since the altercation on the trip back from the county seat.

In those first weeks Rush noticed that Eloise seemed to be getting color in her cheeks. One day as he crossed the yard she spoke to him. Rush halted, admiring her. She was such a pretty thing, tall, slender. And she seemed to be filling out.

"Mr. Vining," she said, "do I smell spring in the air?"

Rush smiled. "Not yet, but soon. It'll come all of a sudden."

A breeze stirred her soft hair. "I'm learning to cook. I have the feeling you didn't think I was capable."

"I think you're quite capable."

She looked away, flushing a little. "I haven't spoken to you since the day you hit that man Bagley. I want you to know again—" She struggled for words. "I just want you to know that my husband didn't overhear the insult. If he had he would have done something about it."

Rush said that he understood. Of course Lee would have confronted

Bagley. He hoped his voice was convincing.

In later days when he saw Eloise she made a point of acknowledging his presence. She spoke or would wave. It made life at Tres Pinos almost bearable in those days.

But as spring approached, Rush felt an incipient explosion hovering over the range. Most of the time Zack was uncommunicative. All he got out of Lee was a cold nod, and the old man spent more and more time in his wing of the mud-walled house. And Rush certainly couldn't bring up his problems to Eloise; she had enough pain already. Some nights he had overheard Lee shouting at her.

All Rush could do was bide his time. In a matter of weeks it would be roundup. Then Charlie Magee would be forced out of his shell. And perhaps by that time Lee would thaw.

Much preliminary work was necessary prior to roundup. Rush was gone nearly two weeks with three of the new hands, making a circuit of the northern boundary of the ranch. Zack said he wanted to make sure Comanches hadn't run off any beef.

Purposely Zack avoided sending him to the south sections of Tres Pinos where a confrontation with the pair at the horse camp might blow the whole range apart. And Rush knew that now was not the time for a showdown with Zack. Zack wouldn't be pushed into getting rid of Bagley and Tinker. Zack had resented the fact that Rush fired them. One truth Zack had voiced; the best way to get him to do something was to tell him he couldn't.

The day Rush returned from making the northern circuit of Tres Pinos he swung down tiredly and saw, a short distance away, Eloise Magee apprehensively eyeing a bay mare Vic Peden held for her. Today she wore a short coat and a trailing skirt and her face under the mass of fair hair seemed quite pale. Paden, the horsebreaker, was trying to argue with her in his quiet way. Then he saw Rush and seemed relieved.

Sensing a crisis, Rush hurried toward

Eloise and the mare. The horse stood with head down, apparently docile, but Rush detected a quivering of muscles under the sleek hide.

"You planning to ride this horse, Mrs. Magee?" Rush asked.

The tall girl seemed to lose some of her paleness. "I'm so glad you're here. Perhaps you can settle the argument. Lee says the horse is gentle—"

At that moment Lee approached, leading a chestnut. "It is gentle," Lee said defiantly. "It's a mare and—"

"No sign it's a good mount for an inexperienced rider." Rush was weary from long hours in the saddle, in the company of men he didn't like. With Zack's gradual replacement of the old crew there was no longer the familiar cameraderie. Whenever Rush brought it up, Zack reminded him that he was only a segundo.

Rush continued, "And I assume you are inexperienced, Mrs. Magee?"

"I—I did a little riding in Baltimore—"

Rush turned to Peden. "What about this horse, Vic?"

"Not half broke to saddle." The horse-breaker gave Lee a sidelong glance. "I tried to tell him."

Rush took the reins and mounted the mare. For a few moments it seemed to settle, its head drooping.

Lee said triumphantly, "I told you it was gentle!"

But at that instant the mare suddenly exploded. It swapped ends and sunfished, then buck-jumped the length of the yard, raising dust. By using his spurs and a strong left hand, Rush finally controlled it. He rode the sweated mare back to the east end of the yard.

"Never have I seen a horse so brutally handled," Eloise said quickly, as if to take attention from her husband. Her lips were pale as she pointed at a reddish froth at the mare's muzzle. "Disgraceful."

Rush wasn't fooled. Dismounting, he turned to Lee. "You trying to get your wife killed?"

After witnessing the wild ride, Lee

seemed subdued. "I just didn't realize—"

"These aren't eastern riding horses." Rush took some of the sting out of his voice. "You have to show them who's boss. Or they'll maim or destroy you." It took supreme control not to backhand Lee across the mouth for endangering the girl's life. "We'll find a gentle horse for your wife. But in the meantime—"

Lee seemed to realize that Eloise stared at him with a strange intensity, as if waiting for him to stand up to Rush.

Lee did. "One thing to remember, Rush," Lee said, the brief humility gone, "you're not the owner of this ranch. Even though you do act like it at times!"

Then Lee muttered something under his breath, swung aboard the chestnut and rode away.

Eloise stared after her husband who was just disappearing into the cottonwoods. "It wasn't necessary to humiliate him," she said, turning on Rush.

"I had to prove that the mare was

dangerous for a woman to ride. Peden knew it but he's only a hand—"

"You're not, of course. You're a partner."

"You resent your father-in-law making me one."

For a moment her manner held, then the stiffness went out of her shoulders. "I don't resent it. I—I guess it's a strain for Lee and me. It's hardly what either of us expected."

"You'll get used to things," he said gently. Peden led the mare into the corral.

"I think in eight years Lee had forgotten what the frontier is like." Muscles in the column of her white throat contracted as she swallowed. "And I guess I never realized the enormous emptiness of the West."

"That's the way a lot of us like it."

"Do you know that after we reached St. Louis the journey west seemed endless? We rode and rode and rode. And I —I think I was frightened every mile of it."

Slowly she walked up to the house,

dust squeezing from under the heels of her trim boots. He stood watching her, an old familiar dream taking shape in his mind. Then it quickly dissolved. She was Lee Magee's wife, after all.

Rush washed up and was ready to go to the cookshack when Lee entered his quarters without knocking. This discourtesy annoyed rather than angered Rush.

"Don't ever again degrade me in front of my wife." Lee brought into the room with him a raw odor of whisky.

"That wasn't my intention, Lee . . . look, this is a time of tension. The worst time of the year in the cow business. Winter's sliding to a close. And we've got roundup to face in a matter of weeks. It's not something a man looks forward to. I hope you and I can ease the strain between us before that."

"The strain is on your side. Not mine!"

"We'll have a lot of work to do," Rush went on patiently. "Work that we'll do—together."

Lee wiped a hand across his mouth, watched a spider pick its way across the sill of a narrow window. He took a deep breath, shuddered and said, "Oh kee-ryst, how I hate this place. I understand my mother hated it. And Eloise—I should never have brought her out here. She's a sensitive girl."

Lee whirled away, slamming the door behind him.

One day Charlie Magee said, "Rush, we need replacements for the remuda. I don't feel like makin' the long trip this year. Take Vic Peden. Go get us seventy-five head." The old man bought horses only from his old friend Raul Castillo, far to the south.

Rush tried to form up a protest in his mind. A cold wind swept across the yard. Just when a man believed spring might be over the hill, winter struck again.

"Wouldn't hurt to buy closer to home this year," Rush said. "I mean, I should stay here."

"I need to get the reins back in my hands. I want to handle things while you're gone. And I'm still tough enough to do it."

Rush considered further argument, then looked down into the faded eyes of this man who had witnessed much of the history of Texas. "Charlie, when do you want me to leave?"

Charlie Magee said morning would be soon enough. "I been watchin' you, Rush. You ain't afraid of Zack, are you?"

Rush weighed his reply. "I like Zack. But I'm not afraid of him."

"You're a good man, Rush."

"Charlie, I haven't had a chance to talk to you lately. Maybe this is the time to bring up something—"

"I know what you're goin' to say. But I want my way in this. For one thing, Lee has set his butt around the house too long. While you're gone I want him to work under Zack. It's what the boy needs. Backbone." The old man paused. "Lee's got to learn to face up to things. If I decide it's time for a showdone, I'll see that him and Zack handle it."

"I don't think Lee is ready for that

kind of showdown. You mean Bagley and Tinker, of course—"

"I'm still the boss here, Rush." It was the old-time voice of Charlie Magee that of late had been strangely troubled. Then he added in a more reasonable tone, "You go do what I told you. Nothin's goin' to happen till roundup. You'll be back by then."

Rush was gone nearly a month. With the help of four Castillo vaqueros he and Peden pushed the seventy-five head of half-broken mounts to the Tres Pinos horse camp at Oatman Springs. The camp, consisting of corrals and a bunkhouse and blacksmith shop, was over twenty miles south of the headquarters place. It was Rush's first visit since Bagley and Tinker had been rehired.

The squat, black-haired Bagley was mending harness when Rush arrived.

Bagley's right cheek was still not healed. "I was drunk that morning," he said grudgingly. "Never should have said that about Mrs. Magee."

"Zack tell you to apologize?"

Bagley's dark eyes were dangerous. He said nothing.

Rush was unimpressed. He saw Tinker beyond the bunkhouse, working on a broken corral gate. Tinker did not look up. It was noon. Rush knew he should stay overnight and rest up. But the hell with it.

Instead, he left Peden to work on the rough string and headed for headquarters. For the first time he noticed that the day held a measure of warmth, and over the Del Carmens the sky had lost the metallic blue of winter.

It was nearly dark when he cut in beside the main house, heading for the corrals. Eloise, wearing a pale blue dress, was near the veranda. She saw him and waved a greeting.

"You're back," she acknowledged as he dismounted, then quickly added, "Rush, do you know what I found today?"

As she looked up at him he felt a melting sensation deep in his breast. It was the first time she had used his first name.

Catching his wrist in her warm fingers, she drew him to the cottonwoods that grew beside the house.

"Green leaves," she whispered, pointing upward.

He could barely see them in the approaching darkness. Someone lighted a lamp in the house and a yellow glow stained the windows.

"And look," Eloise said, her voice excited. She pointed at a stem of weed pushing up from the hard Texas soil. "You don't know what it means to see something green."

Then she seemed to realize that she still held his wrist. Flushing, she stepped back.

"This country agrees with you," he said. "You're prettier than ever."

"I'm glad you're home. It wasn't the same with you gone."

"Everything all right while I was away?" he asked quietly.

She nodded her golden head. "Lee is

adjusting to ranch life. And so am I. Lee and Zack have become friends. I'm sure that will please you."

"Of course." Rush was glad for the darkness so she couldn't study his face too closely. "I'd better go and clean up."

He found Zack seated at the desk in their quarters, a deck of cards held in one large hand. He was dealing himself a poker hand.

Zack got a tight grin on his lips. "How's all the *putas* down in Laredo?"

"No time for girls on this trip, Zack." Rush sailed his hat to the antler rack. "I see Bagley and Tinker are still at the horse camp."

"You surprised?" Zack drawled, watching him.

"I hoped they'd be gone by the time I got back."

"I got more news for you. Oro Lance is goin' to run one of the roundup camps for us."

5

RUSH felt heat in his cheeks. He was too weary for argument. And yet it was up to him to take a stand against Zack. Just as he was about to unload he remembered that, after all, Charlie Magee was the boss. And if the old man hadn't seen fit to question Zack's hiring practices, what was a segundo supposed to do about it? He was reminded of Eloise saying how her husband and Zack had become friends, a strengthening of ties between the Tres Pinos heir and the foreman.

When Rush returned from the cookshack with a pan of hot water for shaving, Zack still played with the deck of cards.

"Gettin' my fingers in shape," Zack said with a grin. "Figure to win money tomorrow. The last Saturday before roundup. And you know what that means."

Rush was honing his razor as Zack began to laugh.

"Rush, you look solemn as a hangin' judge."

Rush's patience wore thin. "You know damn well this is wrong. To hire men the old man doesn't like." Rush examined his reflection in a triangle of looking glass on the wall. He could see Zack glaring at the back of his head.

"I had it out with Charlie," Zack said, his good humor slipping away. "I hire who I want."

That evening Charlie Magee made one of his rare appearances at the cookshack for supper. He seemed glad to see Rush home. He inquired about his old friend Castillo and Rush told him the Mexican enjoyed good health. During the meal Rush avoided mention of Oro Lance because Zack sat across the table. Rush half expected the old man to bring it up. He didn't.

When supper was over Charlie got up from the bench at a long table where some of the men were still eating. "Rush, walk up to the house with me."

Zack, on his third cup of coffee, jerked up his big shaggy head to stare.

Rush walked out into the quiet, star-filled night. He and the old man walked in silence for a few paces in the direction of the lamplighted windows of the main house.

"Rush, reckon you know what tomorrow is." And when Rush said he did, the old man continued, "Will it hurt too much if I ask you to miss out on the fun?"

"What do you have in mind, Charlie?" Down at the corrals some of the horses were snuffling."

"For one thing, Lee can't hold whisky."

"Time he learned maybe."

"There's people in town who don't like me. And they just might take it out on Lee. If I get too drunk to notice." Charlie halted. "Rush, keep Lee here. Even if you got to tie him."

"What if he objects?"

"Now that's a damn fool question. Seein' the size you are." Charlie gave a dry laugh. "I'll tell Lee you'll show him parts of the ranch he ain't seen yet. Ride him around all day. Don't bring him back till dark. We'll be gone by then."

"It won't set well with me giving him orders. Better if you told him."

"He'd pay no attention to me." The old man touched Rush on the arm. "Do this one thing. I'll never ask another favor."

Rush didn't like it.

"I've treated my boy worse'n a Comanche treats his dog. I figure it's time I make things right."

"Charlie, there are some things I want to bring up—"

"Never mind that," Charlie Magee snapped. "Just give me your word you'll keep Lee here tomorrow."

"You've got more of a reason than worrying about some possible drunken trouble in town."

"Startin' next week things may be some different around here, Rush."

"How do you mean?" Rush gave the old man a close look. "You'd better let me go to town with you."

Charlie's face hardened in the wash of house lights. "This is how I want it. I still own Tres Pinos. And I run it!"

In the morning Lee was waiting for Rush at one of the corrals. As if in defiance he wore in place of range gear one of his black eastern suits. Rush was reminded of Zack's comment: Lah—de—dah.

Lee showed little interest in the parts of the ranch Rush tried to show him. After eating the lunch the cook had put up for them, Lee drank from a flask, then grudgingly offered it to Rush. Rush shook his head.

When they were riding again, Lee said, "I'll want to change clothes before going to town tonight. And don't mention it to Eloise."

"Saloons are a part of life for a man."

Lee gave an embarrassed laugh. "I'm talking about the building in back of O'Hale's. Zack mentioned it."

69

"Zack should keep his goddam mouth shut."

Lee's mouth was white as he jerked around in the saddle. "You've got no right to cuss Zack."

"I'm thinking of your wife is all. Those women—"

"Sometimes you act like sweet purity personified. At least I never shot a man half to death."

"I suppose Zack also told you about that." They were climbing a brushy slope.

"It slipped out once when we were playing poker. That by-play between you and the sheriff that day in Wheeler. I understand it now."

"Good old Zack."

"Maybe I shouldn't have brought it up." Lee rode close and forced a smile. "These days it seems I have an urge to hit back at most everybody. Let's forget what I said, huh?"

Rush made sure they got home before sundown. He didn't like the idea of Eloise alone at the ranch. There had been no more talk of Comanches, but renegades were not necessarily copper skinned. They came in all colors.

When he passed the house Rush saw Eloise at a window and felt relieved.

As he and Lee rode to the nearest corral, Rush commented on the deserted yard. "Everybody went to town ahead of us."

Lee swung down, then said, "Rope me out a fresh horse."

His tone stiffened the short hairs at the back of Rush's neck. "Lee, you're not going to town."

"Just who in the hell says I'm not?"

Rush exercised a maximum of patience in explaining that it was Charlie Magee's decision.

Lee doubled his fists. "Why, you son of a—"

"Careful, Lee!"

"This is your idea. Not my father's—" With a cry of rage, Lee swung at Rush's head, then stepped lightly aside. Rush went after him, took a stinging blow to the jaw and another that snapped his head back.

Lee danced, fists lifted. "I'm an experienced boxer," he jeered. "One thing I do well, Rush, my friend."

Youthful, agile, he glided in again. Rush let him swing at his face.

Ducking, Rush snapped, "You poor damn fool. Don't play fancy with me!"

Rush lost his temper. Catching Lee by the shoulders, he spun him completely around. His backhand caught Lee across the side of the face, driving him against the corral wall.

Eloise came running. "Are you trying to kill him?" she gasped. "What is the meaning of this outrage?"

"Listen to me—"

"You're a man of violence!" Her blue eyes were bright with anger. "I thought as much that day in Wheeler." She panted from the long run down from the house. "The sheriff asked my father-in-law if you had been behaving yourself. Indicating that you had been in trouble before. And then you struck Bagley. Oh, he probably deserved it. And now you turn on my husband."

Lee rubbed at the mark on his face left by Rush's backhand. "I'll tell you what the sheriff meant. When Rush was nineteen he shot a man. The man was lucky to live."

Rush winced at the way Eloise looked at him, the anger in her eyes replaced by loathing.

"I'll tell you the facts," Rush said wearily. "In case Zack neglected the rest of it."

"We're not interested," Eloise told him.

"You'll listen," Rush snapped. "I raised horses. To pay my way through school. I sold some horses to a man. He refused to pay, thinking I was too young, too inexperienced to make an issue out of it. I went after him for payment. He tried to kill me. I shot him. I spent a year in jail."

"If the man had died," Lee said, his voice no longer touched with anger, "they'd have hanged you."

"How awful." Eloise seemed shaken. "Thank God he didn't die. For your sake." Something glistened in her long pale lashes. "Why did you fight with Lee just now?"

Rush told her.

"But why would Lee's father object?" Eloise was surprised. "Lee's certainly old enough to drink with the men."

"The last drunk before roundup," Lee said. "A tradition in these parts. A last chance for the men to let off steam."

"Charlie doesn't allow any whisky at roundup camp," Rush explained.

Then Lee seemed to lose the last of his vehemence. "Rush, I shouldn't blame you for what happened just now. It's the old man—He keeps at me until I don't seem to have any sense left in my already addled brain."

Rush stared at him in surprise.

Eloise said softly, "I would like for the three of us to be friends." A breeze had come up, stirring her long skirts. "I baked some honey cakes today, Rush. Will you gamble and eat one with us?"

Rush glanced at Lee. Lee nodded and Rush said, "I don't think it will be much of a gamble." She had mentioned friendship. All of a sudden this seemed most important to him.

After caring for the horses, Rush walked up to the house with them, where Consuelo served beef and chilis. The talk was mostly of the coming roundup. When they ate cakes and drank coffee before the big stone fireplace, Rush felt the need to repay Lee for accepting blame for the brawl.

"You can handle your fists. You almost had me down."

Lee gave a bitter laugh. "You handled me as if I were a child."

"Rush is bigger than you," Eloise pointed out. "You shouldn't have tried to fight him."

"Maybe I wanted to erase my streak of yellow—"

"You're *not* yellow," Eloise protested.

"—Or perhaps I secretly hoped Rush would beat me soundly. So that I couldn't ride a horse for weeks. Then I could sit in the house and forget about this damned ranch. Or maybe it was something else."

"Lee, don't talk about it," Eloise said with a strained laugh. A log crackled on the hearth.

Lee said, "Rush, we'd probably get along. If the old man were out of the picture. But I do think he's right about me not going to town. If I did, I might give him heart failure. Sometimes when he looks at me I have the feeling he's either going to vomit or drop dead."

Eloise gasped. "Lee, don't say such a thing."

"Every time he looks at me he sees my mother. That's why I got out of here when I was a kid."

"My own father was killed when I was seven," Rush said. "I never got to know him, not really. I envy you, Lee, having yours."

"You're welcome to him," Lee said with a harsh laugh.

Eloise sat stiffly across from the leather couch Rush occupied with Lee, her pretty face showing strain in the lamplight. They nibbled at the honey cakes. From the kitchen came subdued sounds of Consuelo on some project of her own.

To ease the awkward silence that had fallen between them, Eloise talked of her early life in Baltimore, how her parents had not survived the war. "One thing Lee and I have in common. We were both raised by an aunt."

Lee gave a shaky laugh. "At least it's one thing we have in common."

Rush finished the cake and complimented Eloise on her first culinary effort. She gave him a wan smile. Rush said he had to get some sleep. As he walked down to his quarters he decided not to be satisfied with Lee's apparent acceptance of his father's order to stay away from town. He just might take it into his head to make the trip alone in defiance, when he thought Rush was asleep. Rush stayed up till nearly midnight to make sure Lee didn't try it. . . .

In their bedroom, Lee stared at his wife's bare shoulders. "Know what I was about to say when we three discussed the brawl?"

Eloise was sitting on the big bed, brushing her long golden hair. "Lee, I'd rather forget about it."

"I was about to say that maybe I secretly hoped Rush would beat me to a pulp. And that you would fling yourself upon my poor lacerated body."

"Don't say things like that."

"If a man can't have a woman's love, perhaps the next best is her pity."

"Do you wish I'd leave? I can, you know. I'm not afraid to travel alone. Not now, I'm not. I've learned many things since I've lived here—"

"No, I don't want you to leave." He crossed the room and placed his hands upon her bare arms. "I'm sorry I said that. I shouldn't have."

6

EVEN though it was long past midnight, O'Hale's Saloon in Pilot Gap was still packed with men, some singing drunkenly, others making a show of card playing. Some were tipped back in chairs along the far wall. One of these, Deputy Sheriff Jim Boomer, hands resting loosely on his fat belly, snored lustily. Two men had passed out on the dirt floor of the long narrow building with its smoky wall lamps, the haze of tobacco smoke.

At one end of the crowded bar, Zack Henley reflected on the fact that Lee Magee's absence had made it a most unrewarding night. All Zack had been able to win at poker was seven dollars from one of Ben Fairfield's TT riders.

Several times during the night Zack caught Charlie Magee giving him curious sidelong glances. But Charlie didn't worry him. Hell no, things were too big for that kind of worry.

He had the feeling it was Charlie's orders that had kept Rush and the kid from joining the crowd tonight. Zack had hoped Lee would bring his pretty wife and leave her in one of the rented rooms up at Lake's wagonyard. Zack thought it wouldn't be unseemly—if Lee got drunk enough and the old man was looking the other way—for him to stroll up and see how the young lady was making out. No harm in that, was there? Zack felt his blood warm, and it wasn't from all of O'Hale's whisky he had put away that night.

Zack's imagery concerning Eloise Magee fell apart when Oro Lance crowded in beside him. Up the bar Charlie Magee narrowed his gaze at Lance, then continued a briefly interrupted tirade against local horse breeders.

Ben Fairfield, chunky, red in the face, shouted, "I got better hosses than that greaser friend of yours Castillo—"

"I don't like that word," Magee snapped. "And you know it!"

Fairfield stalked away, with Charlie cursing him in two languages.

Lance helped himself to Zack's bottle. "Sounds like the old man is getting drunk."

"I wish he'd get dead."

Lance turned his yellow-flecked gaze on Zack. "I still say the kid bringing home a wife kind of upset things."

"You had a chance to finish things at the wagon camp out of Wheeler. Why did you let Rush bluff you out?"

"It wasn't quite the time to see that the old man fell off a wagon seat. Or to let a wheel run over him, or the team run away."

"Bagley and Tinker were there," Zack snarled. "How much help did you need, for kee-ryst sake?"

"You're whiskied up to your eyeballs or you'd know better than to talk that way to me."

Zack turned his head, but Lance's dark face was smiling.

"Well, I reckon the gal being along did ruin things," Zack agreed. "If she hadn't been there you could have got Rush and Lee off chasin' Comanches. Leaving the old man behind. But with the gal—yeah, it sure changed things."

"Rush didn't believe that Comanche story I spread around Wheeler. I could tell that by the way he acted."

"Rush is smart. Too smart, mebby."

"I still say, forget this so-called friendship. Shoot him in the back of the head and be done with it—"

"Any shootin'," Zack said thinly, "I'll be the one to do it."

Lance tasted his whisky. "I tried my damndest to make friends with Charlie when I rode into camp that evening. You can't fault me there. But that damned Rush—"

"With that rattlesnake temper of yours," Zack grunted, "it's a wonder you didn't cut him into eight pieces. Before he even had time to reach for his gun."

"I thought about it," Lance said with a nod of his head so that the laced gold piece on the chin strap swung across the front of his black shirt.

"A lot of things can happen at roundup," Zack said in a low voice. "Charlie Magee's last foreman ended up with a ladino horn in his gut. Funny if the old man went the same way."

"Or a horse could fall on a man. Or a steer jump him. Or he might get tangled up in his own rope and be dragged."

Down the bar, O'Hale, thin black hair greased over a shiny pate, perspired as he set out bottles for the noisy crowd. In addition to matching drinks with his customers, he had to listen to Charlie Magee yell in his old man's voice how much cheaper he could buy whisky across the river.

O'Hale was relieved when Charlie finally shouted, "In ten minutes Tres Pinos rides home! Drink up, boys!" The old man lurched toward the winter doors that were still up. Then as his drunken cowhands began to finish their drinks along the bar, he called to his big foreman. "Zack, see you a minute?"

Zack followed him out to the shadowed walk where the horses of the various outfits were lined up at the hitch rails. No lights showed in the few residences of the settlement. The business district was one long block with the wagonyard at the east end. Across from the saloon was Kane's Saddle Shop and some empty buildings, behind which was the one-room jail. Next to O'Hale's was the Great Texas Store.

From Pilot Gap to the east stretched a forbidding area of thorny brush and deep canyons. To the west it was equally bleak; over there was Tres Pinos, then the river and Mexico. A country where a man could have his throat sliced for a 'dobe dollar, his horse stolen, or his hair lifted in those infrequent times when young bucks broke out of the hated reservation and roamed south from Indian Territory to seek vengeance against the pale skins. To ride once again under the Comanche Moon of their forbears, to avenge those long ago crimes against their womanhood, the years when any female Comanche above the age of nine was fair game on blanket or Texas hardpan.

To the west there were Mexicans who could never forget San Jacinto. And all around were Texans who found the Alamo easy to recall after a night of drinking. Sometimes the first Mexican they met became the object of that memory. The Mexican population of Pilot Gap, meager as it was, had dwindled under the threat of belated retaliation for a massacre. It was at this point that Charlie Magee took most of his business to the county seat up at Wheeler.

Zack towered above Charlie Magee on the walk in front of O'Hale's. At the edge of the walk the thick dust had been turned to a muddy stain by those drinkers too lazy to push through the jam and out the rear door to the privy O'Hale kept for his patrons.

Charlie stood looking up at the sky, filmed by clouds that dimmed the stars. Not even a hint of a later moon; the night black as a roofed-over hole in the ground, was the way Zack put it.

In the saloon the Tres Pinos men cursed because the long night was coming to an end. And now all they had to look forward to was roundup. Weeks of it. And no whisky. Kee-ryst!

And as the Tres Pinos men began at last to make some show of leaving, one of the two women who stood in the doorway of a small frame building behind the saloon muttered, "Thank God, they're going home."

"Thank God nothin'," said the second woman. "Count your money and be thankful for Tres Pinos."

On the walk out front, Zack said, "Good thing we're pulling out now, Charlie. Last year we had to tie you to the saddle. Remember?"

Charlie Magee turned from a dark contemplation of the sky. He tilted up his small, tough face with its gout of white beard. "I ain't one bit drunk, Zack. Took a long time for me to chew this over tonight, Zack."

"Chew what over?"

"But when I seen you an' Oro Lance

with your heads together, I figured it out. Rush was right all along. And I shouldn't have give you so much rope to string out. But I wanted to see just how far you'd go."

"Charlie, you're talkin' wild—"

"I should've kicked you out when you put Bagley an' Tinker back to work. Then hired on Lance—"

"Good cowhands are hard to find, Charlie."

Charlie Magee gave a squeaky laugh. "Cowhands? Hell, they're gunhands. You tried to bait a big fat hook with a honey-cake. I didn't swallow it." The old man dropped a small leather sack into Zack's hand. The contents made a faint clinking sound.

"What's this mean?" Zack stared down at the sack.

"Five hundred in gold. More'n you deserve. Two years you worked for me. In some ways you been a good foreman. In others you ain't worth a damn."

"Charlie, you better cut this talk—"

"I figure you changed about the time

you heard Lee was comin' home. Before that you thought I'd die one day. And you'd just kind of take over Tres Pinos. That Lee would stay east. And mebby you'd send him a piece of money now and then. To keep him quiet. Ain't that how you figured it, Zack?"

Light from the saloon was reflected in Zack's hard eyes. "You're loco, Charlie."

"I could have had Rush take care of this. But I always been a man to do his own dirty wash. I'm doin' it now."

"Jeez, Charlie. You an' me been good friends."

"You're to get out of Texas. Don't even come to the ranch for your gear."

"You can't kick me out," Zack said, his rage starting to shred the last of the forced good humor. "Hell, you forgot my fifteen per cent."

"Soon's Flannery gets back from Austin I'll have him fix up papers so Rush gets your share. He's earned it."

"Rush has put you up to this," Zack accused, trying to find out just how much the old man actually knew about things.

"I sent Rush south 'cause I didn't want him to maybe stumble onto your game. And you'd kill him. You see, I got some mighty fine friends across the river. Sometimes I get word about what's goin' on over there."

"You can't take the word of a greaser —word of a Mexican."

"Tres Pinos cows been showin' up fifty head at a time over there. Brand worked from a Three Pines to Three Diamonds."

"The hell you say."

"Know the reason I held off shoutin' about it?"

"I'd like to hear it."

"Because at first I thought Lee was in on it with you. Stealin' from his own poppa. Only because he wants to go East and I won't give him the money. But now I know he ain't got the guts for such a bloody game. No, you're in it yourself, Zack. You and Lance and them other two."

"You're so sure, why didn't you swear out a complaint with Jim Boomer?"

"Because this is the easy way. Take the

five hundred. I ain't never heard of a cowman payin' a bonus to the thief that stole from him. But then I'm an odd cuss in a lot of ways."

"That you are."

"I want you to get out and leave Rush and my boy to run Tres Pinos. I don't want either of 'em hurt. I know my boy couldn't stand up to you. And I wouldn't want to gamble that Rush could and live. So you clear outa Texas. You ever come back I'll see you hung to the nearest tree. I mean it, Zack."

Charlie Magee swung aboard his big sorrel, backed it away from the hitchrail, then leaned forward so he could see through the dirty front window of the saloon at the mass of drunks.

"Come on Tres Pinos!" he shouted. "Shake a leg. We're goin' home!"

Slowly the old man rode up the deserted, shadowy street, waiting for his men to stagger out to their horses and catch up to him.

Oro Lance slipped out of the saloon. "Zack, what's up?"

"The old bastard fired me." Shoving the leather sack into his pocket, Zack glanced into the saloon. Men were starting to head for the doors. Without a word Zack leaped aboard his own horse. He spurred it savagely away from the rail, heading up the street in the direction taken by the old man.

By the time the first of the drunken Tres Pinos hands reached the walk, Zack and the old man had been swallowed up in the shadows.

These were the ones to hear Zack's strident cry far up the street: "Hold him in, Charlie! Hold that loco hoss in! *Hold him!*"

Men on the walk stiffened, heads swinging in the direction of the shouting, the sudden rattle of hoofbeats up there in the dust. And the sounds of a horse snorting wildly. A sudden gunshot ripped through the town.

The slam of the gun was something their liquor-fogged brains could seize upon. Some broke for the alley. Others attempted to shove their way back inside, against the outward pressure of the men who tried to push to the street in order to see what was going on. Drinks were spilled; a bottle fell from the bar, gurgled its way across the dirt floor as it rolled under a deal table.

O'Hale, big hands resting on the bartop, pale saloonman's face turned toward the street, cried hoarsely, "My God, what's happening out there!"

And when no shots followed the first, they all broke for the street. Those already outside were weaving up the street, some of them stumbling. They picked themselves up and staggered on. . . .

7

RUSH would never forget that day. For him it started a little after four in the morning when one of the Tres Pinos riders pounded into the yard.

"It's the old man!" he shouted to Rush. "Saddle turned on him an' his hoss spooked. He was drunk as hell. The hoss killed him." The rider paused for breath while Rush stood frozen in the doorway to his quarters. "Zack says for you to bring the kid an' his wife. Funeral's to be early this morning."

When Rush awakened the Magees and related the grim news Lee turned white. Eloise cried, "How awful."

While Rush hitched a team to a spring wagon, Eloise slipped into the first dress she could find, donned a cloak and came down the yard with Lee. Saddle horses would get them to town quicker than a wagon. But Rush did not want to put the girl to the test of riding a mustang all the way to Pilot Gap. Besides, what was the hurry, Rush asked himself. The deed was done.

The three of them rode in silence across the brushy flats now stained with moonlight.

By the time they saw the first lights of Pilot Gap, the stars had started to fade. A grim-faced group met them and muttered condolences.

Town ladies took over Eloise, exchanging glances of disapproval at the yellow dress worn by the tall girl. *Yellow*. Was she so callous as to ignore tradition?

In O'Hale's, Lee sobbed against the bar. Zack tried to comfort Lee with whisky. And Rush listened to the story of the tragedy told by at least twenty men. All witnesses, they said. But he knew this part of it wasn't true. In questioning them, he learned that most had been in the saloon, only three or four on the walk. And up at the end of the street where it had happened the shadows between buildings had made the street dark as a tunnel.

Charlie Magee, after a night in the saloon, had carelessly neglected to properly cinch up his double-rigged saddle. And had the further misfortune of having picked a skittish horse to ride.

"Hoss went crazy at somethin' that blew across the street," Zack explained. "Before I knew it, Charlie was under the hoss with one foot still in the stirrup. I had to shoot the goddam hoss." Zack whapped Lee Magee on the back. "Have another drink. In honor of your poppa. He was a fine old man." Zack looked defiantly around the mass of silent faces, as if daring anyone to sully the memory of such a sainted personage as the late owner of Tres Pinos.

Rush's stomach turned over. He drank a whisky. It did not dispell the sickness in his belly, only put a fire to it. Around him men talked in quiet tones and a few of them actually mentioned the departed's good points. Although it seemed a strain. Once the last spadeful of dirt landed on

Charlie's coffin, Rush knew the soft-voice praise would end.

Charlie Magee had been a small tough man in a country of big men. "A forgotten corner of God's earth" was how a visitor had once described Pilot Gap and the surrounding country.

At first the country had been ranched by hardy brown men from across the river. But in those earlier days the Comanche had proved most formidable. Now only a few of the tougher Anglos ran cattle and horses, cussed the Yankee government or re-fought the war. And if drunk enough, some of the veterans would exhibit scars from Pickett's Charge or Manassas, or Mayre's Heights or Fredericksburg. They had driven their cattle north to Abilene. And when that town balked at the period of annual violence, trailed further west to Newton and Dodge.

As Charlie Magee once put it: To survive in these parts, a rancher had to be one part lobo wolf, one part diamond back rattler, and eight parts son of a bitch. . . .

In the cemetery, Rush stood on one side of Eloise, Lee on the other. As the interminable dedication to the soul of the deceased to heaven's rangeland continued, Eloise sagged. Rush slung a protective arm about her waist. She briefly slumped against him. Then she straightened, her head high, ready to endure the rest of it.

When it was finally over the town ladies gathered around Eloise and Lee. The men, in a separate group, shaped their hats, cleared their throats.

"Lee try to wear his pa's boots," one of them remarked, "and he'll have to grow some."

"One of them big Yankee outfits could probably buy Tres Pinos purty cheap."

"He better sell. He can't hang on."

Rush turned his face up into the sun; a warm spring morning that Charlie Magee had never lived to see. "Lee will make out," Rush told the men. And added in a louder tone, "Zack and I will see to that."

Zack, standing nearby, threw a large shadow across the graveyard fence. "Reckon we will," he agreed.

Rush walked over to where Lee and his wife were stepping away from the town ladies. "Are you folks ready to go back to the ranch?"

Eloise nodded. She started to draw her traveling cloak across the front of the yellow dress. Then as some of the town ladies stared, she let the cloak deliberately fall away.

"I know what you're thinking," she said in a dull voice. "I didn't stop to think to wear black."

"Forget it," Rush said. There hadn't been time enough to send to the ranch for a suitable dress before the funeral. And because she was taller than the other town women, to have borrowed a dress would have been out of the question.

On the way back to Tres Pinos the three of them rode in silence, wedged in the seat of the wagon. A spring breeze touched the girl's pale hair.

Finally Lee said, "I can hardly believe that Poppa is gone."

Rush made sure his voice betrayed no inner turmoil. "Charlie was an old man. He'd had a long life."

"It just doesn't seem possible—" Eloise seemed choked up, "possible that it was an accident."

Rush tensed, wondered if he should comment, then decided this was not the time. He kept his eyes on the dusty wheel tracks that cut across the rolling country.

Lee spoke to his wife. "You have to remember that my father was in his seventies. He was—well, why deny it? He was dead drunk. And he tried to ride a horse while in that condition."

"And the saddle conveniently turned on him," she said, her voice shaking.

"It was an accident." Lee sounded exasperated. "Everybody says so. Zack had to shoot the horse, remember. He thought he was saving my father's life."

"I don't blame Zack for any of this," Eloise said.

Rush noticed that her long slender

fingers closed into fists against the lap of the yellow dress.

She continued, "Zack has been most kind. But I'm wondering if some enemy of your father's—perhaps someone wishing to gain control of the ranch—could have done something to that saddle. Or paid someone to do it."

Rush was aware that her eyes raked the side of his face. "If you mean me," Rush snapped, "say it."

"I just don't know what to believe."

Once when they dropped into a dip in the road she slumped against him and he felt her softness. The scent of her hair clung briefly and then was lost in the stinking greasewood smell as the horses tromped on brush growing at the edges of the narrow road. In the distance, a coyote alerted by the approaching team loped into the spring grass.

To make conversation, Rush said, "We'd better hunt some of those coyotes. They can kill a calf if they gang up on it."

Neither of the Magees replied.

It was a long tense drive back to the ranch. In the yard, Eloise brushed past her husband and ran to the house, her long hair streaming down her back.

Lee stepped down. "Don't pay any attention to what she says. She's all broken up."

Rush tied the team to a stump. "I think it's time you and I had a discussion, Lee."

Lee looked irritated. In three months, since his return to Tres Pinos, the Texas sun had barely started to erase his eastern paleness. "Rush, I want to get a drink and take a nap. Whatever you have to say can wait—"

"I want your permission to fire Oro Lance." He added Bagley and Tinker to the request.

A familiar stubbornness settled over Lee's handsome face. "It's Zack's decision. He's the foreman."

When Lee started away, Rush caught him by an arm. "You better listen to me —"

"Lance is a friend of Zack's. Which

makes him a friend of mine." Lee pulled away from Rush and stalked into the house.

Rush led the team to the nearest corral where Vic Peden, the bow-legged horse-breaker, sat on a bench. Peden used the point of a Tennessee pea sticker to dig a pebble from a crack in his bootheel.

"Too bad about the old man," Peden said gravely. He put the knife in a sheath at his belt. "I just heard about it when I come up from the horse camp."

"A damn shame." Rush started to unharness the team.

"I hear his saddle turned on him," the older man said carefully. "That how you figure it, Rush?"

"For now I figure it that way," Rush said significantly.

"Old Charlie could ride a hoss through a cholla fire while standin' on his head. I can't figure him forgettin' to tighten a cinch. Drunk *or* sober."

"Were Bagley and Tinker at the horse camp last night?"

Peden shook his head. "They went to

town. Would've gone myself but these days whisky an' my guts don't mix. . . . You reckon Lee would make out with the old man dead?"

"I intend to see that he makes out." Rush unbuckled a harness strap. "How you feel about it, Vic?"

"Lee ain't much. But the old man treated me fair. I'll string along with you, Rush."

"How many of the crew can we count on?"

Peden stared thoughtfully at the leafing cottonwoods. "Can't rightly say. With them changes Zack's been makin' here and there."

"It's the way I figure it." Tres Pinos used a full time crew of twelve. Beginning with roundup and lasting till winter, the crew was enlarged to thirty men.

That evening Rush was in his quarters when Zack walked in, the floor creaking under his weight. "Should've stayed in town," Zack said, giving Rush a sidelong glance. "We had a regular wake for the old man." Zack walked on over to the desk, big belted gun jogging at each step. He sat down heavily. "When I rode in just now I heard Lee and his woman arguin'. From what I could make out she don't think the old man died accidental."

Rush thought it over and decided for the present to play it easy. "You know how women get crazy ideas."

"How you feel about Charlie gettin' killed?"

"I wasn't even there—"

Zack locked thick fingers behind his neck. "But you do take my word for what happened."

"You were with him. You should know how it was." So that Zack couldn't study his face too closely, Rush crossed the room to adjust the lamp that had started to smoke.

"Every man in O'Hale's said that's how it happened," Zack said. "Even Jim Boomer, who I admit ain't got brains enough to pack into an acorn shell."

"Boomer adding his voice makes it official."

"Now let's settle somethin' else,

Rush." Zack unlocked his fingers and leaned forward. "I postponed roundup for a week on account of the old man. When it's over, then we'll talk about Oro Lance. I know that's chewin' on you."

Rush fiddled with the lamp. "I suppose Lee has told you I think we should fire the three of them."

"One thing to remember, Rush. You're only the segundo around here."

Rush wheeled, clenching a fist. Zack's blunt warning to keep his place, added to the other pressures, almost caused Rush's temper to go. But as he saw big Zack glowering at him from across the room, it struck him like a blow in the face that if he tried for a showdown now it could mean the end of everything.

"I'll remember," Rush said, and let the tension run out of the fist he slowly unclenched.

The next two days Rush, prodded by desperation, tried to talk to Lee Magee. But each time he went to the house Eloise met him at the door to say, "Lee is ill, Mr. Vining. Please don't bother him."

Rush would turn away, knowing very well the source of the illness. Worst of all, he couldn't even reach Eloise. She had stopped using his first name. Apparently the old man's death had erected a wall between them. He found it hard to believe that she could suspect him of complicity in Charlie's murder. And murder it was, what else?

He even considered riding the long miles to the county seat for a talk with Sheriff Tom Faulkner. But what evidence did he have? And would the sheriff even listen if Rush did have reasonable proof? Faulkner would never quite forget that six years ago Rush had put a bullet in the left breast of a larcenous second cousin of the sheriff's. No, Faulkner would likely twist any facts Rush might bring north with him so that no action was taken. Either that or twist them so that Rush himself became involved. Only the fact that Charlie Magee had been a power had kept

Faulkner off the neck of one Rush Vining this long.

Charlie Magee summed up his own evaluation of the lawman one day when he said, "Faulkner must have a taste for leather. The way he's always lickin' my boots."

Tensions mounted daily at Tres Pinos. Rush was given what he termed senseless chores. Zack kept him on the move; hunting down a band of coyotes and later a lobo pack spotted by a Mexican goat herder. Zack made a point of keeping him away from the horse camp. And even Oro Lance put in no appearance at Tres Pinos headquarters.

Four days after the death of Charlie Magee, Zack ordered Rush to take the big wagon to town and load up with supplies for the roundup camps.

In Pilot Gap, McGregor, who owned the Great Texas Store, said, "It's about time Tres Pinos did some local business. All this thanks to Zack."

Rush made no reply. While the wagon was being loaded, he climbed the outside stairway of the store building to the office of Flannery, Charlie Magee's lawyer. But the office was locked. A hand-printed note tacked to the door said Flannery was in Austin on business.

Outside in the bright sunshine, Rush looked toward the graveyard on a distant rise of ground. "Charlie, whoever did it to you will pay," he whispered. "This I promise."

8

RUSH started for O'Hale's, dodging a boy rolling a barrel hoop along the walk. Of the two horses tied at the rack, one bore Ben Fairfield's TT brand. As Rush quietly entered the shadowed building, he realized that the half dozen men knotted at the far end of the bar were discussing the late Charlie Magee. Rush stood for a moment, his back to the doors.

". . . and Charlie stole every section of land he ever owned. Stole half the cows he threw his brand on. I'd like to drink a toast to the hoss that killed him—"

O'Hale was the first to spot Rush. He went pale, cleared his throat and said loudly, "Hiya, Rush."

There was an abrupt silence from the men who had been downgrading Charlie Magee. Apprehensively, they stared at the tall man in the doorway, hat on the back of long brown hair. And they seemed to notice a steel brightness in his eyes. Some of them even lowered their gaze to the cedar-butted .44 at his belt as if realizing for the first time that he always went armed.

To them he had been just an easy-going cowhand that Zack Henley had insisted be hired on at Tres Pinos before Zack would agree to act as foreman. Just a segundo who acted as a kind of flunky for Charlie Magee, while the real running of the ranch was done by Zack. But now they seemed to read a new toughness in his manner. In the new hardness of his face, the slant of his gun. And the way he now looked at each of them in turn, with contempt. Perhaps some of them remembered that over east he had once nearly killed a man in an argument over a sale of horses.

Ben Fairfield, who had been speaking when Rush entered said, "All right, I ain't ashamed of it." The ruddy broad face bore a deeper flush than usual. "I said it to Charlie's face many a time."

Slowly Rush walked down the bar where O'Hale nervously set out a bottle and glass. Even a fly bumping crazily against a tin reflector of one of the unlighted lamps seemed startlingly loud.

With a steady hand Rush poured himself a drink. "When Charlie Magee started ranching here," he reminded, "it was the custom to appropriate anything that could walk. And to haul in a wagon anything that wasn't nailed on tight or fastened too deep in the ground."

Fairfield, half drunk, glared at Rush. Two years ago he had tried to augment his raggedy-pants cow activities by raising horses. He had tried to sell some to Tres Pinos. He had never gotten over Magee's refusal to do business with him.

"Loves a greaser more'n his own kind," Fairfield had said when Charlie Magee continued to buy from Castillo.

And now in O'Hale's Saloon, the other men standing with Fairfield seemed ready to break for the doors at the first hint of trouble. It was that time of year when the long Texas winter was done. And the tensions and hardships of roundup faced each cowman, big or little.

Rush drank off his whisky. "Charlie had his faults," Rush told them. "But he had fewer than most men."

"Nobody shed tears for Charlie," spoke up one of the men. "Not even his own boy."

"Lee took it hard enough," Rush defended.

"I say one thing," O'Hale put in. "With Zack runnin' Tres Pinos this town will get a lot more business than old Charlie ever give."

"Good old Zack," Fairfield said, and then curled his lip at Rush. "To hear some folks talk—blowin' a big wind around here—you'd think Rush Vining runs Tres Pinos. Instead of Zack and the kid."

Through the window Rush saw Jim Boomer angle down from the direction of the wagonyard. Rush laid a coin on the bar to pay for his drink and went out to meet the deputy.

Boomer paused under the overhang to

wipe his fat face on a bandanna. "Sure was a fine funeral," Boomer wheezed.

"Nothing fine about any funeral. Especially Charlie's."

Boomer lowered the bandanna. "What do you mean by that?"

"Why didn't somebody keep Charlie from trying to ride a horse? If he was so drunk as everybody claims."

Boomer seemed relieved. "Oh, that. I was thinking there for a minute that you figured there was something funny about the way he got killed. I hear Lee's wife has been making talk."

"Just an unfortunate accident," Rush said. "Everybody drunk. I suppose even you, Jim."

"Oh, I'd had a few. But I sure wasn't drunk. When Zack went out with him ahead of the others, I figured—well, I figured Zack was trying to talk him out of riding. You know, Charlie could get so drunk he had to be roped to his own saddle." Boomer made another pass with the bandanna across his sweated face.

"But I reckon Zack couldn't tell him nothin'."

"So it would seem."

"You know Charlie was mule-headed and if he figured to ride a hoss home he would do it."

"Charlie was stubborn," Rush agreed and watched the deputy's face.

"Zack will do a lot for Tres Pinos. Lee is sure lucky to have him."

"Maybe." And Rush knew from the way Boomer's mouth hung open that he shouldn't even have said that much. But his nerves were approaching a dangerous point of strain. He felt like a man attempting to walk a greased wire across a thousand foot canyon. One misstep and it could be the finish.

"I tell you one thing, Rush," Boomer said, stowing the bandanna in a hip pocket, "you shouldn't talk against Zack. You'll need friends now that you ain't in the old man's shadow. As a matter of fact, the sheriff already passed the word for me to keep an eye on you."

"Adios, Jim." Rush got away before he

let the whole thing slip out of him. Not only would he endanger his own life, but Lee's. Perhaps even Eloise, depending on how much risk the high stake players were willing to take in this bloody game. Already they had risked much. Charlie Magee was dead.

As Rush drove the loaded wagon out of town he mulled the problem over in his mind. To the south a buildup of thunderheads dimmed the intense blue of the sky. Somehow he had to get Eloise to take Lee to the county seat for a talk with the sheriff. Either that or Rush knew he faced the moment when he either killed Zack or died by Zack's hand. And to down a man of Zack's obvious popularity could result in a hanging. Rush experienced a chill as he pictured Sheriff Faulkner wearing a black suit, escorting him to the gallows.

When Rush got home he ordered the wagon unloaded, the supplies stored in sheds. Later, chuckwagons would be brought up from Oatman Springs, loaded and then dispatched to the first of the roundup camps. The hands sullenly obeyed his orders.

As he left the wagon, Rush saw Eloise sitting on the west side of the house, brushing her long hair in the late afternoon sun. It was the first time he had seen her out of the house since Charlie's death. Finding her alone was luck.

She heard his step, looked around and pushed a sheaf of golden hair away from her face. "Mr. Vining, I've just washed my hair," she said coldly. "It is a time when a woman wants privacy."

Rush fought an urge to catch her by the arms, shake her. Force her to listen to him. Making sure no one eavesdropped at the two narrow windows on this side of the house, he sank to his heels beside the stool where she sat.

"I have a favor to ask," he said earnestly.

"Just what favor?" Her voice was unfriendly. Today she wore the yellow dress, sleeves pushed up so that he could see a golden down on her soft forearms.

"Please don't discuss the possibility

that your father-in-law's death was anything but an accident."

A pulse throbbed at her temple. "You disapprove of me. I even sensed it in Wheeler that day. Now you ask a favor. It's presumptuous of you, Mr. Vining, under the circumstances."

"I didn't necessarily disapprove. Maybe I did think that Lee should have learned the cattle business first. And then got married."

"You *are* presumptuous!"

He wondered what had upset her; a quarrel with Lee? The intense dislike so obvious in her large blue eyes cut into Rush's own temper, her senseless antagonism burning through him like the raw whisky he had taken that day in town.

"And besides learning how to ranch first," Rush snapped, "I considered this to be one hell of a place to bring an eastern woman to live."

"You say eastern as if it denotes a weakness." Her bosom was stilled against the front of the yellow dress.

"This is tough country, ma'am," he said stiffly. "You have to be tough to survive."

"I'll survive, Mr. Vining."

He sank back on his heels, his face on a level with her own. Gradually his anger drained away. "I thought we were beginning to get along. I'm sorry I lost my temper."

She looked away. "I was beginning to like you. To feel I could trust you."

"And now you don't. Because somebody's put ideas into your head."

"I don't know what to think."

"Is Lee feeling better? I mean well enough so I could talk to him."

"You know as well as I that his illness —" Her voice caught. "He's been drunk since his father's funeral." She squeezed her eyes shut. "Why did we ever come out here? Lee tried to find employment back home. But I don't know—" She made a vague gesture with the silver-back hairbrush. "Nothing seemed to work out. Then he said we should come here. That Tres Pinos was rightly his."

She fell silent. Rush stood up, seeing the sunlight touch one side of her face and the sheaf of long damp hair that fell across her shoulders.

"I'm asking you, please, let me handle things," Rush said quietly. "And don't mention Charlie's death. Not unless you pretend to agree with the accepted version."

She looked up at him, her eyes searching.

"And don't tell anyone of our talk," he went on.

"Does the anyone mean Lee? Or perhaps Zack?"

"I didn't mention names."

A small frown appeared between the large eyes. "My father-in-law spoke so often of your great friendship with Zack. And now you seem almost to resent him. I've noticed the way you look at him lately." She sprang up, the hairbrush gripped in her two hands. As if making up her mind to something, she said, "Lee is much better today, thankfully. Perhaps

119

in the morning you and he could have your talk."

"I'm counting on it."

Eloise nodded, then hurried into the house.

9

THAT evening Zack failed to appear at the cookshack for supper. Rush ate with the crew—beef, beans and stewed tomatoes. Occasionally he caught the men watching him and felt their resentment. It was understandable; Zack had hired them. And Zack had probably made no secret of the fact that Rush had preferred the old crew.

Finished eating, Rush stepped from the cookshack and heard Zack's booming voice reach him from the main house.

Rush looked in that direction. In the deepening twilight he saw a glow of cigars on the veranda.

Zack called out to him again. "Rush, come on up and set for a spell!"

As Rush approached the veranda he could made out Lee and Eloise and Zack sitting on the veranda. And with them, smoking a cigarillo, a tight, arrogant smile on his dark face, was the gunman, Oro Lance. Rush felt a coldness along his spine.

"Mighty fine meal, Eloise," Lance said smoothly, the yellow-brown eyes not on the girl, but on Rush there at the foot of the veranda steps. "Wasn't it, Zack?"

"Mighty fine," Zack agreed. "Rush, that Vic Peden ain't doin' so well at the hoss camp."

Rush tensed. "Nobody better working out the rough spots of a remuda. Peden is the best."

Lee cleared his throat. "Rush, I'll get a chair. Come on and join us."

Lee started to get up, but Rush shook his head. "I've got bookwork to do. Have to figure out how much we owe Castillo for those horses."

"Mr. Vining is not very sociable," Eloise said, a note of strain in her voice. In the twilight her hair was a golden cloud.

Oro Lance leaned forward. "You mean to say that Castillo let you drive horses away from his ranch and not even set a price?"

"Charlie Magee and Castillo were friends." Rush knew Lance was baiting him, but he plunged on, not wanting trouble in front of Eloise. "As a friend, Charlie would set his own price. It would be a fair one. Castillo knew that."

"I'd sooner trust a stepped-on rattlesnake than a greaser," Lance drawled, settling back in his rawhide chair.

"Charlie didn't want that word used on his Mexican friends," Rush said coldly. "I don't like it either."

Zack stood up, huge, shadowy on the porch. "You shouldn't talk to Oro that way. Summer lightnin' is some slower than that boy is with a gun. You oughta stop and think about it."

Eloise said worriedly, "I'm sure Rush didn't mean anything—"

Lee turned on her. "I thought we agreed that under the circumstances you would refer to him as Mr. Vining!"

Zack gave a short laugh. "Rush is actin' like a kid. Pouting just 'cause he wasn't invited up to the boss' house for supper. Rush, you got to remember that a segundo on a spread this size ain't near as big as a foreman."

"So you've reminded me."

"Now you can't expect the boss and his purty wife to invite all the hired hands—"

"Your friend Lance seems to have managed an invitation."

Angrily Rush stepped back from the veranda steps. Something drew his gaze to Eloise. She sat stiffly in her chair, upper body tensed, the eyes so large, the lips thinly stretched across teeth as if locked against an appeal she wished to scream at him.

Swallowing, he turned down the yard. And as he watched the dull pewter look of the stars take on a silvery sheen, he wondered just why he stayed on at Tres Pinos. Because of the share in the ranch Charlie had given him? Because he wanted to avenge what he knew had been a cold-blooded killing?

Or was it Lee's wife? The mute appeal

he had sensed upset him. No, he was only sorry for her. He tried to tell himself that it was the first two reasons that made him stay on here and take Zack's abuse until the time when he could trap his ex-friend into revealing what had really happened on that tragic night in town.

Halfway down the yard he heard Zack's heavy pounding gait behind him. And Rush thought, maybe this is it! He felt a drop of sweat roll down his side and his right hand was so tensed the tendons ached. Slowly he turned.

It was Zack, all right. Zack grinning in the faint afterglow.

"Rush, we've had fun together." Zack seemed serious about it. "Sometimes I wonder if you even remember."

Slowly they walked down to their quarters. Zack lit a lamp.

"Rush, I want you to remember what I told you about stickin' with me. Till we come to that fork in the trail. Then I'll tell us which one to take."

"Why did you take Lance to the Magees tonight?"

"Lee wanted to hear about Mexico. Who better to tell him than Oro?"

"We might as well settle one thing here and now." Rush licked his lips, aware of a pulse going crazy at his throat. "Zack, I'm a partner in this ranch."

"Fifteen per cent ain't no bigger than—"

"A flyspeck on a mule's rump. All right, Zack. But here it is. I know what you're getting at. You mentioned Vic Peden tonight. He's a damned good horsebreaker and you know it. None better. Now here's an ultimatum. Don't fire Vic Peden!"

Rush braced himself as Zack's moon face reddened in the lamplight. "I try to be friends," Zack said almost in a whine. "Remind you of all the fun we've had and now you—"

Rush felt the rest of it gush out of him like storm waters over the lip of a crumbling dam. The hell with it, he thought. He clamped a hand to his gun.

"You're trying to play some underhanded game with that weak-livered Lee. And I won't let you do it!"

"You and Sherman's army?"

"Just me, Zack!"

And he saw Zack's big hand come to rest on the ivory butt of the gun he had won from Oro Lance in a cantina in Monterrey. How Rush and Zack had laughed about it. Oro paying a Mexican to carve the figure of his sweetheart on the grip. And then losing not only the gun but the sweetheart to Zack. Lance saying with a twisted grin, "Welcome to her, you black-hearted bastard."

And now in the space of a heartbeat Zack could pull that same gun and blow Rush to pieces.

But Zack dropped his hand away from the nude figure of the woman from Monterrey. He forced a smile, almost as twisted as the one Lance had given when he tried to be good-natured about losing his gun and his *puta*.

"Hell, you and me—" Zack broke off. "We got a lot of ridin' to do yet. We don't want to shoot each other to rags."

Rush felt the tension and the sweat run out of him. For some reason Zack didn't want a showdown. Not yet. Not here—

There came a sharp interruption as Lee Magee hammered on the door, shouting drunkenly.

"He'd even sniff a cork," Zack said, still with that tight grin, "and he roars like *el tigre* at ruttin' time."

Lee weaved in. "Kicked me out, by God," he said thickly. "My own wife." Lee gave them a sloppy grin. "Not really. But I figured we could have some poker."

Zack let a booming laugh rumble from his throat. "Good idea. Come on, Rush."

"Later," Rush said narrowly and watched Zack sling an arm across the shoulders of the new owner of Tres Pinos. They walked together, laughing, to the bunkhouse.

Rush hurried to the main house, knocked lightly on the door, one hand on his revolver.

In a moment the Mexican woman Consuelo, holding a lamp, opened the door.

128

"Si?"

"I wanted to make sure that Senor Lance has left," Rush said in Spanish.

The woman knew what he meant. "That *pelado*. He is gone. He ride—" She gestured toward the south.

"The Señora is all right?"

"In her room. I will tell her of your worry."

"Don't. And *gracias*."

In the bunkhouse Rush stood with his back to the wall, observing the five-handed poker game. For two hours he watched the play. Zack passed a jug regularly. Lee lost forty dollars and had to give an IOU. Rush rolled cigarettes, smoked them, trying to fathom Zack's motives. The big man seemed genial, despite the scene earlier. When Zack caught Rush's eye he would grin. *Compadres* you and me, Rush could almost hear him say. Friends.

Rush directed most of his attention to Lee. To make sure Lee didn't scribble out a quit claim deed to Tres Pinos. Whether that was Zack's plan or not,

Rush had no way of knowing. He couldn't quite picture Zack as being that subtle. It was Zack's nature to let things ride, then make a lethal snap decision and violently end whatever problem he felt needed to be solved.

Finally, when Lee could no longer focus his eyes, Rush said, "Zack, he's had enough."

Rush got Lee to his feet and waited tensely for Zack to challenge him. Zack only smiled and raked in the small pot he had just won.

"Go ahead, walk him home," Zack drawled and tipped back the jug for a long drink.

"And mebby Vining can get a good-night kiss from Missus Magee," said a voice from one of the bunks at the shadowed end of the room.

Rush heard Lee's quick breath and waited, wondering if Lee would react. But he didn't. Somebody snickered.

Turning, Rush stared into the shadows, but he couldn't distinguish faces. "That's enough," he warned, then walked Lee out into the chill spring night, Zack's laughter following them.

As Rush propelled Lee toward the house, with Lee's head bobbing as if tied on with string, Rush began to wonder if Zack wasn't subtle after all. And planned on Eloise being the catalyst.

Rush tightened his hold on Lee's arm. "Don't take one more drink tonight. Not one. You're going to have a clear head in the morning."

"I'm sick—" Lee jerked away, making a horrible sound. And he was sick. Rush waited, struggling against an urge to hit Lee one minute and pity him the next.

At last he got Lee walking again. As they neared the porch steps, Rush said, "Next time Zack tries to get you drunk, tell him no!"

"I drink because I'm afraid of this place." Moonlight touched Lee's wide, staring eyes. He stood on the lower step, which brought him to Rush's height. "I'm so scared I'm sick from it, Rush."

"Don't listen to Zack. Be your own man. And don't break your wife's heart."

"My wife's heart is my business!"

"You walked off and left her alone with Oro Lance."

"Are you implying—" Lee tried to draw himself up, but he swayed and had to reach back to the porch rail for support. "Lance is a *gentleman!*"

A shadow moved on the veranda. "I'll take him now," Eloise said in a shaking voice.

Rush got him to the porch. "Lee, in the morning we'll have a talk."

"I never should have come back to Texas. It killed my mother. She hated it. I hate it!" He screamed the last.

Because Lee seemed on the verge of collapse, Eloise asked Rush to help him into the house. Rush got him to the black leather couch in front of the fireplace. Lee sagged back on it and Rush stooped and pulled off his boots.

Eloise stepped away, beckoning to Rush. Her lips were white. "I overheard you mention Oro Lance," she said stiffly. "I am quite capable of taking care of myself. I am not afraid of him. Or of any man."

"Don't take chances again. You don't know this corner of Texas like I do."

"Are you trying to say that Lance would—" She flushed and looked away.

"I'm not saying he would or wouldn't. I'm only asking you not to run such risks again."

"But surely with Consuelo in the house with me—"

"I'm *asking* you!"

She looked startled in the smoky lamp-light with her husband lying drunk on the couch and the crackle of blazing logs in the fireplace. Rush said gently, "Charlie used to keep a shotgun in the house. Find it. You might have to use it."

"I—I never fired a weapon in my life."

"With a shotgun all you need to do is point it." He walked to the door, Eloise trailing along, twisting her hands together. Rush said, "In the morning we're going to take a long ride. To the county seat. Are you game?"

She looked at him questioningly. "I

also overheard Lee say that he was afraid. Who is he afraid of? Is it Zack? Or Lance? Or you?"

"Will you just do as I ask. *Please!*" Taking her by the arms, he shook her slightly. "It's important that you tell no one about this."

She stepped back, straining against his grip on her arms. And finally he let her go.

"Good night, Mr. Vining."

He tried to measure the depth of coldness in her voice. She did not look at him as he stepped from the house.

10

THE poker game in the bunkhouse continued most of the night. Toward morning Rush heard Zack stumble in and fall into snoring sleep without bothering to undress.

Zack was still snoring when Rush left and hurried to the cookshack for breakfast. With any luck Zack might not awaken till midmorning. Right after breakfast Rush planned to have Lee and his wife meet him at the barn where he would have a buckboard waiting. Rush then planned to drive not to Pilot Gap or the county seat, but to the river. At Los Coyotes there would be vaqueros waiting for roundup to start so they could hire on with the big outfits. Somehow Rush would talk Lee into agreeing to pay for a new crew. Or if Lee had no cash, to at least guarantee their pay. No better riders, no better fighters than vaqueros.

Only then, with a new crew as escort, would he take the Magees north. Once Zack guessed their destination he would be after them. But with a superior force Rush could hold him off.

Once in Wheeler, the sheriff would be forced by the full power of Tres Pinos, as represented by Lee Magee, to investigate the murder of Charlie. Really investigate, not just take the word of a lot of drunks as Jim Boomer had done. Probably Boomer was as drunk or drunker than the rest of them. Surely someone in that crowd at O'Hale's had heard something. The prestige of a sheriff's badge, as opposed to that of a deputy's, might influence reluctant witnesses. At least Rush was counting on it.

And even if this failed, he knew that Zack, if cornered, would eventually be unable to stand pressure and lose all control. With any luck, Zack might give himself away. Rush had observed this trait in Zack. Zack could retain a certain affability until the breaking point. Then everything boiled over in him.

Rush was just finishing breakfast when Vic Peden limped in. One of the little bronc buster's eyes was closed and his lower lip deeply cut. Men looked up as Peden slid onto the bench next to Rush.

"I want my time," Peden said in a low voice.

Rush poured coffee into a tin cup and handed it to Peden. "What is it, Vic?" he asked as the man sipped from the cup, wincing as the hot coffee came in contact with the cut on his lip.

"I won't work with them bastards, Bagley and Tinker. We had words. They beat the hell out of me." Peden put a hand to his side. A broken rib, perhaps, Rush thought. Peden continued, "I got away in the dark. With them after me."

Rush leaned close. "You stick," he said quietly. "I've got some ground to cover today. I want you with me."

"For you I'll do it."

"Grab some breakfast. I'm going to get a wagon."

The minute Rush stepped into the yard he knew he had blundered into something. Beside the bunkhouse wall was Bagley, hat on the back of his greasy black hair, heavy body tensed. In Bagley's big hair-backed right hand was a long-barreled .44, the muzzle on a line with the buckle on Rush's belt.

And in that moment Rush felt something hot and reckless break loose inside. "You beat up Vic Peden. Why?" Rush stepped toward Bagley, as if not seeing the gun. Or ignoring it.

Zack's booming voice from the porch of the main house had the same effect on Rush as a shower of ice water. Making a half turn, Rush saw Zack looming up on the veranda; at his side was a white-faced Lee Magee. Zack was smiling. All of a sudden Rush realized that Zack had only pretended to be asleep.

And either Bagley had come up from Oatman Springs on Zack's orders or had decided on his own to finish the quarrel with Vic Peden. No doubt it was the former.

Zack said loudly, "What's goin' on down there?" And something in the tone of Zack's voice made Rush feel that the foreman knew damn well what was going on. It had all been planned and Lee—stupid Lee—was on hand to witness the final act.

"Zack, let me tell you something!" Rush said in the same loud voice used by his former friend.

Rush did not finish it, for although his words were directed to Zack, his slanted gaze was on Bagley's face. Bagley, still gripping the gun, looked toward the house as if awaiting Zack's further orders. Or to note his reaction to whatever it was Rush had seemed about to tell him.

In that shredded second of time Rush lunged, caught Bagley's thick gunwrist in both hands. His whole weight dragged on the arm, pulling Bagley to the ground. A yelp of pain, a curse broke from Bagley's lips.

Rush twisted hard. Bagley's fingers lost their power and the gun fell to the ground. When Rush tried to seize the weapon, Bagley sprang up and pulled him aside. They collided, then broke apart, rolled.

Rush came up first with Bagley raging, "I owe you somethin', Vining!" And Rush knew he referred to the scar tissue visible at the corner of the left eye.

Men poured from the bunkhouse as Rush made a grab for his belt gun.

Before he could reach it, a weight was suddenly on his back.

Tinker cried, "I got him, Clyde!"

Desperately Rush tried to swing Tinker off his back. But the rawboned redhead stuck like cactus splinters in a saddle blanket. Straight back Rush fell. And before Tinker could pull free, he was smashed against the ground by Rush's weight. Twisting aside, Rush again tried to reach his gun. He leaped away from Tinker who was gasping, the scar in the center of his forehead having the color and the appearance of a finger of bleached bone.

Before Rush's fingers could lock to the grips of his revolver, a dark, arrogant face swam into his range of vision. And striking downward with a metallic glinting in the early sun was the barrel of a revolver. Rush, off balance, tried to duck away from it. But his momentum carried him at a slant into the slashing tube of metal.

In a white burst of lightning the world fell out from under his feet.

Zack lumbered down the yard ahead of Lee. Lon Tinker was on his feet. He had lost his hat and the fiery red hair was grayed from yard dust. Tinker held a Remington revolver in a freckled fist that he pointed at the skull of the unconscious Rush Vining.

Zack grabbed Tinker's arm and warned in a hoarse whisper, "No. Not yet. Not this way."

Tinker looked at him with belligerence and surprise. But Oro Lance, holstering the weapon he had used to down Rush, said, "Lon, he's right. So far so good."

At that moment Lee came up, panting, pushing his way through the ring of Tres Pinos hands. Vic Peden, the horsebreaker, stared down at Rush, started to say something then met Lance's cold eye. He kept his mouth shut.

A flag of dust lifted by the combatants slowly settled back to earth. All the yelling had upset the three horses Bagley, Tinker and Lance had ridden up from Oatman Springs.

Lee looked at Rush lying inert on the ground. "My God, he's dead."

Zack turned to Tinker. "Lon, you take Rush to town. Tell Boomer to lock him up."

And when Tinker nodded, Lee turned on Zack. "Rush needs a doctor, not jail."

"His head is hard as Chisos rock," Zack said. Then he whispered a few words to Tinker that Lee couldn't hear. He caught Lee by an elbow and walked him up to the house where Eloise waited anxiously on the porch.

"What happened to Rush?" she asked quickly.

"He wanted trouble," Zack told

her. "He got it. You two wait in the house."

"Who are you to give us orders?" Eloise demanded.

"I figured that when Charlie died the wolves would move in. They already have. Just do what I say. I'll explain later."

Then Zack walked back down the yard to where men stood around, watching the unconscious Rush Vining loaded aboard a bay horse like a roll of canvas. Zack inspected the lashings, walking clear around the horse. He snatched Rush's hat that Bagley was holding. He stuffed the hat under one of the tight ropes that held Rush to the back of the horse.

"Lon, don't untie this bastard," Zack warned Tinker. "Not till you get to town and Boomer's holdin' a gun on him. You understand?"

"Yeah," the redhead answered and glared at the prisoner, as if recalling their violent encounter when he had tried to help Bagley by climbing Rush's back.

Zack, noticing the look, said, "See that he gets there. Alive. If you cross me on this I'll drive a hot spike through the top of your head. So help me."

Tinker seemed impressed. He mounted. Gathering the reins of the horse that packed Rush, he rode out of the yard.

Zack faced the crew, bellowing orders. Roundup was to start the following day. He ordered the men to head for Oatman Springs. There they were to pick up the remuda and then proceed to the first of the numerous roundup camps scattered across the Tres Pinos range.

Vic Peden headed for the corral with the rest of the crew. The cut on his lip was bleeding again. He kept a bandanna pressed against it.

Just as Zack started to turn away, he saw a chubby Mexican wearing a big hat and a charro vest riding up on a shaggy pony. The Mexican grinned under a thick downcurving mustache.

"Took you long enough to get here," Zack grunted. He led the way into his quarters, the Mexican and Lance trailing along. Zack slammed shut the door and began to talk.

ELOISE felt her heart begin to hammer. She and Lee were in the house.

"What happened, Lee? What did they do to Rush Vining?"

Lee was hunched on the leather couch, a hand over his eyes. "I don't know. I— I just don't know how to cope with these men."

"You're the owner of this ranch. You must assert yourself."

Lowering his hand, Lee gave her a weak smile. "Assert myself to a man with a cannon at his belt?"

"You *are* right. We never should have come to Texas."

"We'll leave. I'll let Zack run the ranch. He—he can send us money when he sells cattle—" Lee seemed elated. "That's it. We'll leave next week. No, tomorrow."

"You're forgetting that Rush is a partner."

Lee's head jerked up. "He and Zack can settle that between them—"

At that moment Consuelo, a shawl over her dark hair, carrying a canvas sack and wearing her town dress, came into the parlor. She seemed upset.

"Señora, I have to go. My sister, she is ill."

Quickly Eloise went to her. "I am so sorry." When the Mexican woman glanced nervously toward the yard, Eloise said, "You're frightened. Why?"

"Sickness. *Malo*, bad. Yes, I am frightened. For my sister and her niños."

Eloise bit her lip. "How could you know about your sister? Who brought word?"

"*Mi tio Hernando*." She gestured toward the yard. Eloise followed the gesturing hand, but saw no one who looked Mexican enough to be Consuelo's Uncle Hernando.

"This uncle has threatened you. He is your real uncle?"

"No. Once he was married to my aunt. But she die. He is—" Consuelo's dark eyes mirrored fear. "I am afraid for my sister. If I do not do as they say she will be hurt. But do not tell them I say this. *Por favor*. Do not tell."

She rushed out the back door. Eloise saw her at a half-trot, heading down the yard, the canvas sack banging against her legs.

At that moment Eloise heard Zack's heavy tread on the porch. And as she turned to bid him enter, he walked into the house. His boldness shocked, then angered her.

Lee said, "Zack, I've made a decision about the ranch—"

"You're not leaving here!" The words tumbled from Eloise's lips. "You're going to fight. As your father would have done!"

Lee looked at her in surprise.

Slowly Zack crossed the room, removing his hat as a grudging courtesy. He slung the hat onto a cherrywood table. The sight of the sweated headgear on

148

polished wood was revolting to Eloise. The table, the only thing left from the furnishings that Lee's mother had brought west with her. The rest of it broken up, piece by piece, and fed into the fireplace "one damn cold winter," old man Magee had once told Lee in defiance and anger.

"Mr. Henley, please remove your hat from that table. There is a rack near the door."

Zack's eyes gleamed, but the thick lips smiled. "Nothin' I like better than a hoss that's hard to break to saddle." And the way he looked at her she knew that he was thinking: or a woman!

Lee looked up and for a moment Eloise hoped he would order Zack from the house. But he didn't. "Zack, what do you think I should do?" His voice was almost a whine.

Eloise felt something come loose inside, like a stone dislodged from a winter slope by encroaching ice. For one terrible moment she almost hated this spineless man she had married. Then she was engulfed with pity.

Zack picked up his hat from the table, hung it on the rack, then came deeper into the room. "Somethin' you folks got to know," he said heavily. He sat down beside Lee on the couch. "Rush is a cow thief."

Lee stiffened. And Eloise felt almost proud of him when he said, "I don't believe it." So many times it had happened, she realized. Just when she thought Lee to be completely without character he would speak his mind as he was doing now.

"And neither do I believe you," Eloise said angrily. "Rush is no thief."

Zack smiled. "I thought Lee said you wasn't to call him Rush no more."

"I did it to placate Lee. You're the one put those jealous thoughts in his head."

"Ma'am, you're sure purty when you're on edge like this."

"What did you do to Rush?" she demanded. "Where is he?"

"Been sent to town. For his own

good." Zack's gray eyes raked her from ankle to forehead and she had the chilling sensation that somehow she appeared before him without her clothes. A heat of embarrassment put flame in her cheeks.

Zack put a thin Mexican cigar between his lips. "Hoped I wouldn't have to tell you about Rush," Zack said in his rumbling voice. "Me an' Rush bein' friends for so long—" He grew thoughtful as if reliving that friendship. Then he gave a shake of his shaggy head. "I've had some of my boys watchin' Rush. It come to a head this mornin'."

"I don't follow this, Zack," Lee said.

"You might as well know that your poppa was fixin' to fire Rush."

"I find that hard to believe."

"When I told you that Rush spent a year in jail you was quick enough to believe."

Eloise gave her own view. "That was different. It wasn't Rush's fault. He told me all about it." She felt obliged to defend Rush. Lee gave her a sharp, questioning glance. Then his mouth tightened in that sullen way she knew so well.

Zack said, "Your poppa found out Rush was stealin' Tres Pinos cows."

"Why didn't Poppa tell me?"

"He was afraid Rush had mebby won you over with his slick talk. Rush was workin' the Tres Pinos brand from three pines to three diamonds. He done it with a cinch ring. Rush is too smart to get caught with a runnin' iron." Zack lumbered to the door and shouted, "Sandoval!"

A chunky, grinning man, who obviously had waited by the front steps, now entered the house. Removing a high-crowned hat, he bowed to Eloise, his lips smiling under a thick mustache.

Zack said, "Hernando, tell Mr. Magee here about them cows."

Sandoval was most glib as he related how he had been offered three hundred head of Tres Pinos cows for two dollars each.

"A fine price," Sandoval grinned. "Very fine. But—"

152

"At such a price why didn't you buy?" Lee asked.

"Señor, I am not a fool," Sandoval spread his brown hands. "The brands, how you say—"

Zack cut in. "He means the brands were so crude a one armed Piute with a sore thumb could've done a better job."

"Why would Rush steal cattle?" Lee asked suspiciously.

"I tell you the truth." Zack glanced at Eloise to see how she was taking it. "Rush has got a gal in Laredo. That's why he talked your poppa into lettin' him go south to buy them hosses. This gal has got princess ideas and Rush didn't have enough money to send her regularly. So he took to rustlin' your cows, Lee."

Zack gave a slight nod of his head and Sandoval bowed, said, "I am happy to help, Señor Magee."

Then he was hurrying down the yard. And as Zack and Lee continued to talk, with Lee disbelieving, then gradually weakening, Eloise saw the Mexican ride out on a sturdy horse. Behind him, on her mule, rode Consuelo, a canvas sack of her belongings tied on behind.

Zack lit his cigar, blew a cloud of smoke. "Lee, you got a lot to learn," Zack said, his voice assuming a paternal note. "And you're learnin' fast. But there's one thing."

"What is that?" Lee sounded confused.

"This is a hard business. A cowman has got to be tough to stay in it—" Zack paused as if what he had to say next was most painful.

Lee urged, "Go on, Zack."

"They claim you ain't got *cojones*. I mean—" Zack glanced at Eloise. "Well, it means a fella with no guts. Although *cojones* ain't exactly guts, if you know what I mean."

"I'm familiar with the word," Lee said, a stiffness returning to his voice. "Don't use it again, please, in front of my wife."

"Sorry, didn't mean that. But here's what I'm gettin' at. You got to make folks in town look up to you. Let 'em know you're as tough a boot as your poppa was."

"Just how do I do that?" Lee asked with a bitter laugh. "Shoot a man in the head? Or hang him?"

"*I* know you're a man, Lee. Damn if I don't. I told your poppa many a time."

"And he believed you, of course." Lee's hollow laughter again.

"You got to town and make them stiff necks know that you're head of your own ranch." Zack's eyes again flicked to Eloise, standing at the end of the couch. "Head of your own house."

"I asked you how?"

"Face up to Rush in O'Hale's. There'll be a crowd around 'cause roundup ain't started yet for most outfits. You tell Rush right to his face that he's fired."

"My God, I couldn't do that. Rush might—" Lee ran the tip of his tongue over pale lips.

"Tell him. To his face. Be a *man!*"

"I—I just don't know," Lee faltered.

"You're boss of Tres Pinos, boy. Show every man in town that you won't have anybody in the pay book that stole cows from your poppa."

"What if Rush denies stealing the cattle?"

"There's two hundred head across the river at Sandoval's place. You tell Rush that. If he's still got guts enough to bluff, we'll take him over there. And let him see that we ain't foolin' one damn bit."

"Will Rush go to prison for this?"

"Naw. You just tell him to get out of Texas. That if he comes back he'll have his neck roped to a tree." Zack looked over at Eloise. "Ma'am, don't you figure Lee oughta show everybody he's man enough to fire a thief?"

Eloise stood with her hands clenched so tightly she felt the ache clear up her forearms. A worm of fear wriggled deep inside. Rush was gone and he was hurt. And where else could she turn? If ever in her life she needed courage it was now.

"I don't understand any of this," she said.

Zack's teeth snapped down on the cigar he smoked. "Understand this then. I'm tryin' to save your husband's ranch for him, Mrs. Magee. If he don't show he's

156

got sand, the wolves will really move in on us. This ain't no eastern lah-de-dah country. This is Texas. And in a lot of years there's more blood falls on the ground than rain!"

Lee said quickly, "Don't talk of violence around Eloise. It makes her feel faint."

And she thought, violence? Since my arrival I have heard or seen little else. My indoctrination came at Wheeler when they talked of the Comanche and what they did to women. And later there was Bagley with the side of his face ground off from Rush's fist. And my father-in-law dying tragically. And Rush Vining this morning in the yard—.

Zack was talking earnestly to Lee about the business in town. It took Zack fifteen minutes to finally convince Lee that he was man enough to fire his own segundo.

When the matter was settled, Zack said good-naturedly, "Lee, I'll see that your wife don't want for company while you're gone. I'll come up and take supper with her—"

157

"If Lee spends the night in town, I go with him," Eloise said.

Zack, on his feet, turned and bent his large head to study her a moment. "If that's how you want it, Mrs. Magee. I'll have Bagley drive you to town in the wagon."

"Lee can drive," Eloise said quickly.

Zack shook his head. "I ain't lettin' you off this ranch without a man bein' along." Zack must have realized how it sounded. He looked at Lee, then added, "I mean, not without *two* men along."

Zack waited while Lee got his coat. Eloise hurried into the back part of the house, saying over her shoulder, "I may be a few minutes. I'm going to change my dress."

In the bedroom she quickly knelt and from under the bed drew out the ugly shotgun with the short barrels that Rush had told her to find. She had located it in the bottom of a chest containing discarded clothing. Now she studied the weapon, trying to decide if she could bring it to town with her.

Lee was shouting from the parlor, "Eloise. Hurry up."

Because the gun would be so obvious for her to carry, she pushed it back under the bed. Putting on her long gray cloak, she joined her husband and Zack in front of the house. There they waited until Bagley drove up in a spring wagon.

She didn't want to sit next to Bagley. She made Lee ride in the middle while she sat on the outside, clinging to the seat brace.

All the way to town Lee and Bagley barely spoke. When they did, it was only to comment on the weather or the coming roundup. Or the condition of the spring grass. Neither of them mentioned Rush Vining.

Bagley took his time and it was mid-afternoon when they finally reached town and drove to Lake's wagonyard, which afforded the only accommodations for overnight guests.

Lake, a taciturn man, was pitching hay for a bull team. He came down and listened while Lee told him they wanted

159

a room for two. Lee helped Eloise from the wagon, then glanced at Bagley. "I suppose you'll want a room?"

Bagley shook his head. "I got to get back for roundup. You can rent a rig from Lake here when you're ready to come back to the ranch."

Lifting a hand to them, Bagley drove out.

In a small, dusty room with a narrow bed, Eloise sank tiredly to a chair. "How much safer I feel in town," she sighed.

"I tell you one thing," Lee said. "I feel more confident than I have for a long time."

"Because of Zack. He's influenced you since the day we arrived at Tres Pinos."

"Zack is a pillar of strength. I realize it now. And to survive I've got to not only depend on him, but trust him."

"Lee, do you know that Consuelo suddenly left today? So frightened she could hardly speak?"

"We'll get another woman—"

"Lee, I think Zack had something to do with her leaving. She mentioned an

Uncle Hernando. And I distinctly heard Zack call that Mexican Sandoval by that name."

"Please, I have enough on my mind as it is." Lee lay down on the bed, a forearm across his eyes.

"Consuelo was forced into quitting. Because she feared some harm would come to her sister. And her sister's children."

"What an imagination you have," Lee said wearily. "I think I'll go down to O'Hale's and—and get my business over with."

"Lee, I think Zack deliberately planned to get Consuelo out of the house."

"Why in heaven's name would he go to all that trouble?"

"Because he thought you'd spend the night in town. That I—I would be alone in the house."

"Zack may be a tough man. But he's honorable. You'll never be able to convince me otherwise."

"Rush warned me to protect myself."

"We'll soon be rid of Mr. Rush Vining,

cow thief and God knows what else." Lee stood, staring vacantly at an intricate overlacing of spiderwebs at a corner of the room. "And I liked him."

"I still like him."

Lee's lips trembled. "How am I supposed to take that?"

"Go on, Lee," she said with a weary gesture toward the door. "Leave me alone. Get your business done."

Lee put his hands on her shoulders. "This is a bewildering country, this Texas. Believe me, I was a boy here. And it has never ceased to overwhelm me. Just when I believe I have a straight trail to follow, it always disappears. And I am left floundering. Trying to find my way."

She touched his hand. "Poor Lee . . . please do one thing. Before you accuse Rush of being a thief, talk it over with that deputy sheriff. Do that for me. Ask his advice."

Lee hesitated, then kissed her lightly on the cheek. "I'll be home in an hour. Then we'll go to the cafe and get something to eat."

When he left the room, Eloise hastily bolted the door on the inside. She wished mightily that somehow she could have brought the shotgun.

Outside of town in a grove of cotton-woods, Bagley pulled up the Tres Pinos wagon. Lon Tinker was sitting on a deadfall. His saddler and the one that had brought Rush to town were tied back in the trees.

"Lee brung his wife to town." Bagley said, stepping down.

"I'll be damned."

"Zack says not to take chances. He'll skin us from ears to heels if the gal gets hurt."

"One thing for sure," Tinker said. "If our plan don't work here in town, it'll sure work somewheres else."

"It better be soon, Zack says."

"It'll be soon."

12

WHEN Lee and Eloise Magee had gone to town in the wagon, driven by Clyde Bagley, Zack and Oro Lance were left alone at Tres Pinos. The men were heading south for the horse camp and then to the roundup camp. Tinker was in town. Even the Mexican woman was gone.

Zack scratched a match on the oak table in his quarters and fired up a cigar. "I think you're right," Zack admitted, puffing the cigar. "We better hunt up Vic Peden."

"He pulled out with the rest of the crew. Should have fired him long ago."

"Lots of things I should've done long ago," Zack muttered, thinking of how saintly Rush had become all of a sudden. Just because the old man had belatedly taken a fancy to him. And that fifteen per cent of the ranch hadn't helped Rush keep his feet on the ground. "Funny, but I figured when we started this little game that Rush would come in with us."

"I read his brand better than you did. I tried to tell you that six months ago." Lance paced the big room that Zack had shared for so long with Rush. "Been a lot easier to get rid of Rush than the old man. You were damn lucky there. I suppose you know that."

"A hit on the head with a gun barrel. The crazy hoss did the rest of it. And with everybody drunk I had time to loosen the saddle to make it look right—"

"My point is this, you should have buried Rush and been done with it. Then we could have let roundup take care of the old man."

"Mebby." Zack stared out one of the narrow windows at the deserted yard.

"And I'll bet that gun you won off me in Monterrey against fifty dollars," Lance said, "that your idea to get rid of Lee won't work."

"It'll work," Zack said coldly. "In

town, if we're lucky. If not, then some-wheres else. Rush will get the blame."

"You're playing this too fancy. Just on account of the woman."

"When Lee's gone, I don't want her to think I had anything to do with it."

Lance toyed with the gold piece on his chin strap. "Know something?"

"What."

"We should've stuck to our original deal. Strip this ranch of beef. Take the eight dollars a head my friends across the river would pay. And clear out."

"That was before I seen Eloise Magee."

Lance curled his lips. "That woman will be the death of you—" Something moved at one of the windows. Glass crashed inward. The round muzzle of a .30-.30 rifle appeared. "Zack! Look out!"

As a rifle crashed, Zack flung himself flat to the floor. Across the room, Oro Lance's right hand was a blur of motion as he drew his black-butted gun. Three shots he sent into the window, smashing out the rest of the glass.

"He's getting away!" Lance cried, wheeling for the door.

"Who was it?"

"Peden!"

Scrambling to his feet, Zack moved with surprising speed for so large a man. In fact, he reached a corner of the bunkhouse even before the rangy Lance. Gun in hand, he saw Peden trying to reach the saddled horse he had left beside one of the sheds.

As that moment, the horsebreaker looked around. He tried to bring up the rifle, but Zack's first shot caught him in the leg. Peden tumbled, losing his rifle. As he drew his revolver and tried to get up off the ground, Zack thumbed two quick shots into his chest.

Peden fell back, his fingers twitching. By the time Zack pounded up, the bronc buster was dead.

Oro Lance came up to stare down at the body. "He aimed to kill you, sure as hell. Lucky I saw him at the window."

"We'll get a shovel. Wouldn't do for the widow to come home and find a dead man in the yard." Zack gave Lance a hard grin, then trotted to the nearest shed for a shovel.

When the body of Peden was disposed of some distance from the barn, where the soil was sandy, the two men rode south to be at the roundup camp overnight, among witnesses, in case the rest of the plan worked out.

13

THE jail in Pilot Gap consisted of one room, four paces wide and six long, with an iron cot and a pail. A tradition of the town was for small boys to gather near the one barred window and pelt the hapless prisoner with rocks. Rush Vining stayed away from the window and the few missles that did enter the cell bounded harmlessly of the stone walls. Twice Jim Boomer came over from O'Hale's and chased the kids away.

"Get away from him now!" the deputy yelled.

Then Boomer would come over to the window and ask Rush if he had suffered any damage. At which time Rush would try and get the deputy to listen to him; to turn the key in the lock of the solid plank door and let him out before blood ran so thick across the range you could wade in it.

"Zack sent word not to let you out till sundown," Boomer informed him.

"Sent word by who? Bagley, Tinker?"

"Never you mind now, Rush—" And Boomer would walk away.

In the late afternoon Rush rubbed at the gash high on his forehead. Only the fact that he had been off balance at the time Lance struck him had prevented a broken skull. As it was, he had been knocked cold as a winter cave.

He had come to on the way to town, turning his head against the flank of the horse where he was tied, cursing Tinker, threatening, then trying to persuade. But Tinker ignored him. At the jail Boomer held a cocked pistol while Tinker cut Rush loose. Even if Rush had wanted to gamble and jump the deputy's gun, he was helpless. So long had he been tied that when he was freed, he slumped to the ground, unable to move. The two of them dragged him into the cell, where Boomer locked him in.

As shadows began to puddle in the

alleyways and the few streets of the settlement, Boomer returned to the jail.

His moon face appeared at the window. "Rush, I want your promise to behave yourself when I let you out."

"Jim, it's time you listened to me. Charlie Magee was murdered. I want you to get word to the sheriff—"

"How come you wait till today to say this?" the deputy demanded.

"Because I thought I could wait for somebody to make a wrong move. That by playing it easy I could get some innocent people out of potential danger. But it's gone beyond that now."

The full impact of Rush's grim pronouncement seemed to finally match the cycle of Boomer's slow-turning mind.

"You claiming Charlie Magee was murdered is the same as calling every one of us that was there that night a liar." Boomer looked indignant. "Now shut your face about it."

"One man committed the deed, not the lot of you."

"Proof you got, I s'pose."

"A powerful hunch I've got."

Boomer gave a shake of his head. "You say one man done it. You tryin' to say that Lee killed his own poppa—"

"I'm talking about somebody who decided Lee shouldn't inherit Tres Pinos."

Boomer's mouth slowly opened. "You mean Zack?"

"I didn't want to believe it either. But I have to."

It took a moment for Boomer to digest this. Then his face reddened. "You're one hell of a friend. If I was Zack I'd kick you off Tres Pinos." Boomer got his second wind and plunged on, his voice shaking. "I tell you one thing, Rush. A lot of folks around here don't cotton to you much. On account of you walked too close to Charlie Magee's shadow."

"Why, damn you, Boomer. You couldn't have got close enough to that badge you wear to smell it if it hadn't been for the old man."

"Sheriff Faulkner wanted a good man here is why I got the job—"

Rush looked him in the eye. "Charlie Magee got you that badge."

Boomer waddled around to the door. In a moment his key made a rasping sound in the rusted lock. The door swung open. Boomer jerked his thumb, indicating Rush was free.

"You won't listen to me, will you?" Rush said, stepping outside. "About Charlie dying."

"It—it just ain't possible. I won't believe it."

Rush looked around into the shadows. "Where's that horse I was tied to?"

"At the livery barn."

"And I'll want my gun." Rush held out his hand.

"It's at O'Hale's. You can get it there."

"Also Zack's idea?" Rush asked quietly.

"Be thankful you get a pistol at all," Boomer snapped, obviously upset by Rush's accusations concerning Charlie Magee.

"Jim, I know the sheriff doesn't like me. And I know why. But he's obliged to do something about this mess. I want to ride with the Magees to the county seat. I'd like you to come along with us."

"Lee wouldn't do one thing for you," Boomer said. "I just come from O'Hale's. He don't feel kindly toward you."

"Lee give a reason for feeling this way?"

"Your name was mentioned and he done some cussin'."

"He's drinking, of course."

"A mite."

"I hope his wife came to town with him. That she didn't stay out at the ranch."

Rush was relieved when Boomer stated that Eloise was waiting for Lee at their room in the wagonyard.

"She wanted to go to O'Hale's with him. Was a powerful argument, according to Amos Lake. But Lee finally put it to her that a lady just don't go to a place like O'Hale's."

"You seen Bagley or Tinker recently?"

"Bagley drove the Magees to town.

174

Seen him heading back toward the ranch."

Rush stared in the direction of the wagonyard that was surrounded by a high board fence. "Jim, the Magees could be hurt," Rush said, turning back to the deputy. "Jim, if you're not going to listen to me about Charlie's murder—"

"It *wasn't* murder!" Boomer was sweating. His wide eyes gave mute testimony that he wanted mightily to believe that it had been an accidental death.

"My point being that you'd better not repeat what I told you. Not unless we both convince the Magees to get out of Pilot Gap and head north. And do it fast. And we both go with them."

"You're the one better keep his mouth shut," Boomer said thinly.

Knowing further argument to be useless, Rush walked away from the jail and along the slot between the saddle shop and the building that had once housed the Mexican cantina. No one seemed to be on the shadowed walks, yet across the street a half dozen horses were at the rail in front of O'Hale's, switching tails in the shadows.

When Rush entered the saloon there was an instant cessation of conversation. Everyone turned to look. Lee was sitting stiffly at a deal table with a bottle and glass. Rush nodded and Lee looked away. O'Hale, just lighting the wall lamps, blew out a match and walked around behind his bar.

Down the bar, red-faced Ben Fairfield said, "Rush, you like our jailhouse any better'n the one you was in last time?" The rancher gave a sour laugh.

Rush ignored the man. Even if somehow he managed to curb Zack's reckless ambition, it wouldn't be easy to continue living here around people like Fairfield. Yet what in the world was easy, he asked himself. For a good many years Charlie Magee had endured the barbs, apparently even enjoying the animosity. Rush looked around the room, seeing the faces in the lamp glow that was beginning to spread along the mud walls and floor, fighting the twilight. Yes, he could suffer through anything this town or Texas itself could throw at him.

If he managed to survive.

"I'd like my gun," Rush told O'Hale, and without a word the saloonman took a belt-wrapped holstered weapon from a shelf behind the bar.

As Rush buckled the weapon around his waist a growing silence in the bar-room seemed most awesome. Every eye was on him. Obviously from Lee's attitude they expected some sort of a showdown between them.

Even though Rush felt the need of food, and his head throbbed, he first had to settle matters with Lee.

He crossed over to the table where Lee was sitting. For a moment Rush watched him, but the younger man refused to meet his eyes. Heeling back a chair, Rush sat down.

He leaned closed, his voice so low that none of those tensely ranged along the bar could overhear. "Lee, in the memory of your father, I want you to get up from this table and leave with me. We'll walk up to the wagonyard together. There we will—"

"Of course you know Eloise is there. I walked up there not half an hour ago, to see if she was all right. Know what she asked first thing?"

"Lee, listen to me—"

"She wanted to know if I had seen you. She seemed most concerned." Lee gave him a twisted smile. "She wanted to come back here with me. To a saloon. My wife in a place like this. Willing to degrade herself only because she worried that you might suffer if she weren't around to protect you."

"Your father once said you couldn't hold whisky. It's the greatest truth he ever uttered."

"I'm surprised you haven't gone calling on Eloise."

Rush waited until he got hold of himself. "Do this one thing I ask, Lee. For all our sakes, come along with me."

Lee got to his feet, weaving, his bloodshot eyes a little wild. "It is my duty—

no, my pleasure, to inform you that your services—"

"Are no longer required?" Rush felt the ache in his head take fire. "Don't play Zack's game."

"Wherever you decide to settle, write to Zack and he will ship your belongings—"

"Settle? I settle right *here*."

"You'd better get out—"

"Maybe it has escaped you, but I am not only an employee of Tres Pinos. I am a partner. Thanks to the generosity of your late father."

"And when my father's lawyer returns to town, I will take steps—"

"You'll take no steps!" Rush sprang up, face to face with Charlie Magee's heir. "For you sake, for all our sakes, I have to play this hand close to my belt. But you might as well get one fact through your stupidly spoiled skull—"

"You can't talk to me that way!"

"—Your father was murdered!"

A gasp went up from the men in O'Hale's.

"Murdered," Rush continued, gesturing toward the front windows. "On that street outside. In this town."

"I refuse to listen to such lies!" Lee cried, and shoved away from the deal table, upsetting glass and bottle. He fled out the front doors.

It was Ben Fairfield who squeaked triumphantly, "Fired you, by God!"

Hardly had the double doors swung closed than Rush was crashing through them. A dozen paces from the saloon entrance, Rush caught Lee.

"Get away from me!" Lee cried, his face drained of color.

"Lee, you're going to listen to me if I have to—"

Frantically Lee made a grab for something under his coat. But Rush's hand was already holding a gun. A moan of terror burst from Lee when he realized Rush had beaten him to the draw and was ramming a gun muzzle against his stomach.

"One thing Zack better damn well teach you," Rush said through his teeth.

"Never draw on a man unless you intend to kill him!"

With one hand Rush grabbed Lee by the arm and shook him so hard that a small, gentleman's revolver tumbled to the walk. Rush kicked it aside. Men were sticking their heads out of O'Hale's front door.

"Get back inside!" Rush cried and gestured with his gun. They ducked and the doorway was clear.

Only then did he holster his weapon and make one last attempt to talk sense to Lee. "We are going to take a long ride," Rush said, trying to get a measure of control into his voice. "We'll pick up your wife and try and—"

"Keep away from me, you goddam cow thief!" Lee screamed. Twisting aside, Lee made a frantic dive for the revolver Rush had kicked along the boardwalk. But Rush caught him by an arm, swung him around, lost his hold. Lee spun backwards, off balance. He fell heavily against one of the posts that supported the hitchrail. As frightened horses tethered there began to squeal and kick, with blood running from a wound in Lee's head, there came a winking orange-red eye from the roof of the saddle shop across the street. As he was leaning toward Lee, Rush caught the flash of light, heard the thunking bullet gouge the boardwalk. And hardly had the winking orange-red eye died in the twilight, than Rush's own gun sent a blast of sound through the town. Across the street something clattered unnoticed to the walk.

By now the horses had swung hindquarters together in their panic, so that no longer was there a clear view of the building across the steeet. Shouting, men poured from O'Hale's. They came up to ring Lee Magee who was bleeding there on the walk.

Gun in hand, Rush backed to the saloon wall. "Somebody tried to shoot him from across the street!" he shouted at the stony faces.

"Lemme in here!" Jim Boomer cried. He began pawing his way through the ring of men. Seeing Lee with blood on his face turned the deputy white.

Before anyone could say anything a woman knifed through the growing crowd to kneel beside Lee. It was Eloise. At sight of the bloodied face she made a low sound of anguish. Then she turned, looking first at Rush's drawn gun, then up into his eyes.

"Why did you kill my husband?" she asked, her voicy heavy with shock.

"Listen to me!" Rush cried, "The shot came from across the street—"

A roar went up from the gathering, led by the voice of Jim Boomer. "Rush, you're under arrest!"

"A rope!" somebody yelled. "Hang the son!"

As Boomer tried to draw a gun, Rush stepped in. With his free hand he swung hard at Boomer's midsection. Wind and muscle flowed out of Boomer and his fat legs collapsed. He fell back into the crowd.

And in the same instant Rush ducked through a slot between buildings. A shot dug 'dobe chunks an inch to one side of his head. In the alley he found two horses tethered in front of a small building. A woman in the doorway took one look at Rush's tense face there in the shadows, his long-barreled gun. Then she screamed and ducked back inside.

Rush pulled free one of the two horses. He was into the saddle before the first of the braver citizens emerged from the opening between buildings. A rifle cracked a shot that ricocheted off the rear wall of the saloon.

Twilight and a fast horse saved Rush, even though the townsmen did their best to run him down. For the past two years he had had a chance to learn the terrain. Every arroyo, ridge, every back trail and screening of mesquite helped him now.

At full dark and five miles from town, he halted to let the tired horse blow. Far off he could hear the pursuers swinging south, away from him. It wouldn't be long before they gave up and returned to O'Hale's to discuss the incident. Come morning, help would be sought from the sheriff at Wheeler. A posse would be organized. That was when the real trouble would start for Rush Vining.

For one of the few times in his life he prayed, and meant it. Prayed that Lee Magee wasn't dead.

If he lived to be a hundred he would never forget the shock mirrored in the large blue eyes of Eloise Magee. How he longed to return and try to explain. But how could he, with every gun in town against him now?

To take his mind off Lee and the grim future that loomed ahead, Rush struck a match. By the flickering light he examined the brand on the sweated dun that he had appropriated.

It bore a TT brand on its flank. One of Ben Fairfield's cowhands had obviously been visiting in the structure behind O'Hale's. Of all horses, he would have to take one belonging to Fairfield.

In Texas they still hanged horse thieves without benefit of legal proceedings.

Stomping on the match, Rush mounted

and started riding. Somehow he would settle this mess. At the moment, however, he had to admit that the prospects were far from encouraging.

14

THEY carried Lee to the room at the wagonyard where a lamp was lighted. Those men who had not left town in the wild pursuit of Rush Vining gathered around the door, talking in low tones, while Eloise bathed the blood from her husband's face. Already Lee's eyes were open. He looked around dazedly, then looked down at the blood-stains on his clothing. His eyes rolled back in his head.

"Fainted, by God," said Amos Lake, relaying the progress of the patient to those outside.

Eloise examined the cut on Lee's cheek, just below the temple, where it had struck the hitchrail post. The wound, slight as it was, had been a bleeder.

Eloise carried a pan of water stained from her husband's blood out to the yard. She emptied it beside a trough while explaining the extent of Lee's injury.

The men exchanged glances, cleared throats, some of them probably realizing that before the true state of Lee's condition could be ascertained they might have hanged Rush or shot him to death. It was a sobering moment.

"Anyhow," O'Hale said, "Rush will be in trouble for assault on Lee. Even if he didn't kill him."

"And he stole one of Ben's hosses," put in another. "That's trouble enough for any man."

Jim Boomer rubbed his soft chin. "I just can't figure what happened. Them two gunshots and—"

"One sounded to me like a rifle," O'Hale admitted. "Damned if it didn't."

"Wasn't no rifle," another scoffed. "Rush shot at Lee twice. Missed both times."

Boomer shook his head. "Not Rush. If he aims at somethin', he hits it."

"Might be he was just trying to scare Lee."

"If that's the case, he done a job of it. Lee fainted dead away at sight of his own blood."

"Sure doesn't have ol' Charlie's guts," O'Hale said. "I 'member one time when Charlie Magee had his finger damn near tore off when he got it caught in a rope. He stood there with his finger hangin', and all he said was, 'Anybody got any whisky.' Jeez, Charlie is likely getting dizzy in his grave. Turning over as much as he must be with Lee—"

"Shut up, his wife is listening."

Eloise, her back stiff, returned to the room and closed the door.

Lee's eyes were open again. As soon as the store opened in the morning, Eloise promised, she would buy him some new clothes. They would burn the blood-stained garments.

Lee had retained some of his color. "Now I guess you believe that Rush is everything Zack claims he is."

"I just hope something hasn't happened to Rush."

Lee sat up in bed. "My God, what kind

of a wife are you? He half kills your husband and yet you have some feeling left for him!"

"Lee, I don't feel like talking about it. You'd better get some sleep."

"Answer me, Eloise."

"Lee, I'm very tired." She lifted the lamp shade, blew out the small flame, then replaced the shade. In the dark she removed her dress, then folded it neatly over the back of a dusty chair. "Lee, I think you were right. This country is too big for you."

"Why this change all of a sudden?"

"Make your deal with Zack and let's go back east."

"You're the one wanted me to stay and fight."

"I'm sick of violence. If we stay it will mean more of it. Perhaps even death."

"You're worried about Rush."

Silently she climbed into bed, got far on her own side and lay with her fingers locked at the back of her head. She always brushed her hair before retiring. But she had no brush. And besides, who would notice? She could hear Lee snoring faintly.

The death Eloise had mentioned came early in the morning—or rather the discovery of it. McGregor, hurrying to open his store, was walking along the south side of the street when he happened to see a rifle. It lay in a slot where the boardwalk did not quite meet the front wall of the saddle shop. Because it was a fairly new Winchester, he halted to look at it more closely. No one would throw away a weapon that was in this good condition. As he bent his lank frame he noticed that the stock was coated with a brownish substance.

Alerted, he picked up the weapon by the barrel. Then he glanced at the front of the shop, seeing several brownish streaks from the roof to the walk.

His mouth flew open. "Somebody get a ladder!" he shouted to the early risers.

Two men finally located a ladder. On the roof of the saddle shop they found the body of Lon Tinker. He had been shot cleanly through the skull, the wound a half inch from the bone white scar in the center of the forehead.

When the body had been lowered to the alley behind the shop a crowd of the curious gathered to stare and to speculate.

Ben Fairfield, who had spent a good portion of the night in the saddle hunting Rush, said, "Looks to me like Tinker was up there to see that no harm come to Lee. Rush spotted him and done him in."

No one seemed quite ready to accept or reject the rancher's theory.

Jim Boomer stared thoughtfully at the body. "A man don't get up on the roof of a building with a rifle 'less he figures to kill somebody," the deputy mused.

Before anyone could question him, he walked up to the wagonyard. Lee and Eloise were just returning from breakfast at the cafe. Lee seemed pale, but reasonably steady on his feet.

"You heard about Tinker?" Boomer asked.

"Damn strange," Lee said.

"Best place for you two is at the

ranch," Boomer said. "We'll rent a rig from Lake. I'll drive you home." Boomer cleared his throat and said heavily, "Besides, I want a few words with Zack."

In the cafe Eloise had heard the news that a dead man had been found on the roof of the saddle shop. At first it had nauseated her to think that Rush—and who else could it be—in this very town had ended the life of a human being. But as she turned it over in her mind, she realized that this was Texas. Here values were different than in the East. Here a man fought for his life. And she was convinced, the more she thought about it, that Rush had saved Lee's.

They were just getting into the rented wagon when Ben Fairfeld stomped up. "Boomer, what you aim to do about Rush stealin' my hoss?"

"Right now I got more important things on my mind," the deputy said gravely and picked up the reins.

"What's more important than catchin' a hoss thief?"

"Catching a murderer, mebby." But

Boomer said it under his breath. He whipped up the team.

Boomer's low-voiced statement did not escape Eloise. But if Lee heard it he gave no sign.

When they passed the saddle shop she saw some townspeople staring at the streaks on the front wall and talking together. Then they turned to stare at the Magees in the wagon. Eloise did not look around at these people who had been so quick to condemn Rush last night.

After several miles on the bright spring morning, she said, "Mr. Boomer, I heard you use the word 'murderer.' Did you mean what happened in town last night? Or something else?"

Boomer's fat hands tightened on the lines of the rented team. "Just turnin' things over in my mind."

"Is it about—Lee's father?"

"Rush told me right out," Boomer said after a moment of chewing on it, "that Charlie was the one made it possible for me to be a deputy. Reckon I knowed it all along. Sometimes a man don't like to face up to things."

"And this has made you decide to—*do* something?"

"I owe it to Charlie—oh, hell—beggin' your pardon, Mrs. Magee—but everything is all mixed up."

"Yes, I agree," she said stiffly.

Lee sagged in the seat, his head resting on her shoulder. "Eloise has finally convinced me we should leave Texas," Lee said.

"Leave Texas?" Boomer seemed astounded. "Why, hell, I mean why— Jeez—Mrs. Magee, I am powerful sorry, but I am just so worked up I can't speak for cussin'."

"Go right ahead. I'm used to it. Out here I guess it's part of the language."

"I heartily agree with Eloise that we should get out," Lee continued. "Zack can run the ranch. But you keep an eye on him, Boomer." Lee gave a feeble laugh. "Just in case."

"You oughta run your own ranch," Boomer told him as the road dipped and climbed; iron rims struck sparks from rocks. "That's what your poppa would have wanted."

"Logic tells me that my first responsibility is to get my wife away from temptation."

"Lee!" Eloise was angered even though Lee tried to pass it off as a joke.

This was followed by an embarrassed silence, with Eloise straightening up in the seat of the jolting wagon, leaning away from Lee so that he could no longer rest his head on her shoulder.

Ahead loomed the buildings of Tres Pinos and she thought hopefully that perhaps Rush would be there. That he would tell her the truth of what had happened last night. But could she believe him? After all, he had once nearly killed a man. And that time he hit Bagley; never had she seen such an explosive temper in a man. At least she had the shotgun under the bed. It was a comforting thought.

As they approached the ranch buildings Boomer grunted, staring at a flurry of activity to the left of the road. "What're them two dogs after?" Then he changed it. "Coyotes, by God."

Eloise and Lee saw the two tawny animals burrowing in the sandy soil some twenty yards from the road. A man's hat lay beside the hole they were digging. As the team approached, their heads came up and they went bounding up a slope and through a screen of mesquite.

Boomer said, "Coyotes that big can pull down a calf. Lee, you better hunt 'em down."

Boomer drove the wagon on across the deserted yard. Two of the corrals were empty. The third one, nearest the bunkhouse, held one mount.

Clyde Bagley stood tensely in the bunkhouse doorway, holding a rifle. "Oh, it's you," the black-haired man said.

Boomer halted the team. "What's happened to all the hosses?"

"Roundup camp."

"Oh, I thought mebby somebody had stole 'em." Boomer looked around. "Zack here?"

Bagley shook his head. "Nobody here

but me. Reckon they're all down at roundup camp. Figure to pull out for there myself. You want me to pass along any word?"

"Your friend Tinker got killed in town last night. Did you know that?"

"The hell."

Boomer studied Bagley a minute, then clucked at the team and pointed them up to the main house. "Zack shouldn't go off and leave only one man to home. Comanches still come lookin' for hosses from time to time. If they can't find any they'll put the torch to everything in sight."

"Talk of Comanches upsets my wife," Lee said.

"I've learned that it is one of the minor problems hereabouts," Eloise said. She turned to Boomer, who was pulling up in front of the veranda steps. "I didn't think Bagley seemed very surprised. I mean, when you told him Tinker was dead."

"No he didn't," Boomer admitted. "I noticed that. Somethin' damn strange goin' on."

Boomer let Lee and his wife out of the wagon.

"Aren't you going to stay?" Eloise asked anxiously. "I'd feel much safer here tonight if you did."

"I'll stay. Tomorrow I'll go down to roundup camp to have a few words with Zack. But right now I want to take a look at what them coyotes was digging up."

He drove down the yard. Clyde Bagley was saddling a pinto. The man gave Boomer a close look as he drove past.

Near the road Boomer tied the team to some junipers. He picked up his rifle from the wagonbed. Crossing the deep sandy stretch on foot shortened his breath. Near a slit in the soil was the hat he had noticed previously, the crown pushed down by sand the coyotes had scratched into it with their digging.

Advancing, Boomer peered down into a shallow grave. His stomach turned over when he saw a small, seamed face. The eyes were open, but partially filled with dirt.

The dead man was Vic Peden.

Boomer took a long breath and knew that he faced a crisis. Well, he had been mighty pleased when a lifetime of failures and disappointment had culminated in the lucky day he received a badge and a deputy's pay. He knew what they thought of him in town; not brains enough to make sense out of a ten foot sign painted on a barn wall, he had overheard somebody once say.

Well, he was going to show them. He was going to show the whole damn range that Jim Boomer had some sand and some savvy.

But he never got the chance. A crackling in the mesquite caused him to look upslope. Clyde Bagley stood there, looking first at the slit in the ground, then at Boomer.

"You're under arrest!" And as Boomer started to lift his rifle, Bagley shot him in the center of the chest.

15

DUST in the early day had attracted Rush Vining's attention. Last night he had camped with some Mexicans herding goats to summer range. After a meager breakfast, he had thanked them, then ridden toward Tres Pinos. With any luck he would find Zack and end this bloody business one way or another. Zack dead or Rush dead.

It was the dust lifted by a team and wagon that caused him to put his horse to a lope. By the time he reached the road and started a cautious approach to the last half mile to ranch headquarters, he saw a wagon swing out of the yard. He saw Boomer's fat figure step from the wagon, carrying a rifle.

Then everything happened with the swiftness of mountain lightning. One moment Boomer was standing, peering down at something in the ground. The next he shuddered and twisted wildly, dropping the rifle. As he collapsed, Rush heard the delayed crack of two gunshots.

Spurring, he finally reached the road and started along it toward Tres Pinos headquarters. Bagley had emerged from the mesquite and started to walk toward Boomer. The sounds of Rush's horse approaching at a hard run caused him to fire one hasty shot, then wheel back into the brushy covering. Then Rush glimpsed him riding hard to the south, bent over the neck of a pinto. Rush was about to try and run him down when he saw Boomer lift an arm from the ground as if to signal him. The arm fell back.

Hastily Rush dismounted and hurried to where the lawman was trying to sit up. As Rush knelt he could tell that Boomer was nearly gone. Someone was approaching on foot. Drawing his gun, Rush looked around. Lee Magee, white-faced, slowed by the barn wall when he saw Rush.

Rush cried, "It's Boomer. Bagley shot him. Give me a hand, Lee!"

He didn't know whether Lee would help him or not: their confrontation in town had been an ugly thing. At least Lee still lived and the only mark on him was a long scratch on one side of his face. Lee was approaching cautiously.

Boomer's eyes flickered open. "Get that bunch of bloody bastards," the deputy breathed. "Zack and the rest of 'em—" A reddish foam appeared at Boomer's lips. With a bandanna Rush attempted to stem the flow of blood from two bullet holes in the man's chest. But it was too late. Boomer's head fell back, he stiffened, then went limp.

Rush threw the bandanna into some weeds. "He's gone," Rush said grimly. He got up and peered into the grave and turned cold when he saw the dead face of the only man he had been able to count on at Tres Pinos. "Vic must have got onto their game. And they killed him."

"My God," Lee breathed, looking down at Peden.

"You overheard Boomer's last words. I guess you know now that it's time to stop this nonsense of stringing along with Zack."

Lee seemed completely shaken. "I—I wonder if they were trying to kill the two of us in town last night?" Lee told him about Tinker being found dead on the roof of the saddle shop.

"I saw something move up there and I fired," Rush admitted. "I didn't know it was Tinker." Quickly Rush questioned Lee as to the number of men at this headquarters of Tres Pinos. There was no one else around, Lee said, only himself and Eloise.

"Still think I'm a cow thief?" Rush demanded.

"If you were, I guess you'd be heading for Mexico by this time."

Rush made Lee help him lift the two bodies into the wagon. Then Rush tied his horse to the tailgate, with the animal rearing, not liking the scent of blood. Rush drove Lee and the dead pair to one of the sheds. There they unloaded the two bodies and covered them with blankets Rush got from the bunkhouse.

"It's the best we can do for now," he admitted, still shocked by the double tragedy. "Lee, I want you to get your wife ready for a trip to the county seat. I wanted to take the time to hire on a crew of vaqueros. But we can't linger that long. Zack will be after us."

"To kill us, I suppose." Lee's eyes were filled with terror. "It just doesn't seem possible."

"We've got to get a move on. Bagley's headed south. He'll find Zack. They'll hunt us down. And with a wagon we'll travel damn slow."

While Lee ran to the house to alert Eloise, Rush got two extra rifles and shells from his quarters. For a moment he stood looking at Zack's bunk, remembering the two years they had shared this room. And before that, the three years he had ridden with Zack to Kansas, to Arizona, Mexico. How far can you ride with a man, Rush thought bitterly, and not know him at all.

In the deserted cookshack he found jerky and cold biscuits, munching this meager fare while he watered the wagon team and the TT horse he had appropriated in town.

Then Rush drove the wagon, with the saddler tied on behind, up to the house. Eloise, wearing her yellow dress, was on the veranda. Her blue eyes seemed enormous in a pretty face drained of all color. She started to move awkwardly across the porch, with Lee helping her. It seemed that her right leg was stiff and she walked with great difficulty.

"What's happened?" Rush cried, springing from the wagon.

Lee was maneuvering her down the steps as Rush tied the team, then hurried to catch the girl by her other arm.

"I heard a great clatter in the back part of the house," Lee panted. "She hurt herself—"

"I fell over a chair," Eloise said, her white teeth clenched. "I sprained my ankle is all. A bad sprain. Very bad."

Rush took her from Lee's faltering grip and swung her to the wagon seat. Lee climbed in after her.

As he picked up the reins, Rush said gravely, "I'm glad Lee is all right. That he wasn't badly hurt. Or dead as you feared in town last night."

"It was a terrible night," she replied in a dull voice.

Rush whipped up the team and they clattered down the yard, past the empty cookshack, the bunkhouse and the lean-to he had shared with Zack. He thought of all that had happened since that first day he had come here with Zack and seen white-bearded Charlie Magee here in this yard. And Zack booming, "Mr. Magee, I'll hire on. But I won't bust up a good friendship doin' it."

And Charlie Magee saying, "I can use a segundo, Zack. Sign him on. To my foreman I'm Charlie. To the rest of the hands I'm Mr. Magee." The old man had looked directly at Rush. "I'm kind of touchy on the subject."

Now Charlie was dead, along with an inoffensive fat man who had tried to play deputy in a country too tough for him. Also dead a loyal horsebreaker named Vic

Peden. Rush felt a raw anger at the savagery. Magee's son could be next. And Lee's wife—

"I want to get one thing straight," Rush said as he shot a glance to the south, saw no hint of dust and felt relieved. "We're running for our lives. We've got extra rifles and shells in the wagon bed."

"Let's pray we won't have to use them," Lee muttered, hanging on as the wagon jolted its way over the terrible road.

Rush cleared his throat. "And Mrs. Magee—"

"Yes?" She turned her golden head.

"I didn't want to take the time at the ranch. But when we make a rest stop, I'll turn my back. I suggest you remove that shotgun you've got strapped to your right leg."

"How—how in the world did you know!"

"I lifted you into the wagon, remember? You had considerable more heft than usual, as old Charlie would say.

208

And I hope to God you didn't load that thing."

Eloise put a hand into her dress pocket and showed him two shells. Then she began to laugh, almost on the verge of hysteria. "And I thought I was being so clever."

"Damn resourceful," Lee was angry. "Seems to me that you could have told your own husband. That story about falling over a chair—"

Eloise got hold of herself and wiped her eyes on a small hankerchief. "Rush, I think it's about time you started calling me Eloise. We've been through a lot together. I suspect we'll be through a lot more."

She glanced at the sky. It was very blue. The guns of spring, she thought, and shuddered.

16

CLYDE BAGLEY intercepted Zack and Oro Lance as they were heading north from the first of the roundup camps. There they had spent the night, Zack still of the opinion that if they had any luck at all in town last night, it would be wise to have plenty of witnesses see them at camp. This part of it had worked, for some of the smaller outfits were already moving into adjoining camps for the cooperative roundup.

But when Bagley related the happenings in town, Zack knew it had all been a waste of time. His mood was black. When Bagley told of the violence that morning at Tres Pinos, Zack's mood was blacker.

"Even the goddam coyotes are against us," Oro Lance muttered.

"The hell with it," Zack said thinly. "Main thing now is to catch up with Rush and the Magees."

"With the way things have changed," Lance said, "what do you figure to do about the girl?" They started riding again, the three of them, heading north toward Tres Pinos.

"I'll make a good squaw out of Eloise," Zack snapped. "In Mexico I'll have plenty of time."

"How you figure to run Tres Pinos from there?"

Zack's broad face was ugly. "We go back to our original deal. We strip Tres Pinos of every damn head of beef we can lay hand to. We peddle the herd to your friends across the river."

"That's the plan we should've stuck to," Lance said angrily. "Instead of you getting ideas about marrying the widow. And running Tres Pinos like a Texas cowman."

"The widow I'll have yet. I'll leave her across the river till we finish our business here. With Rush and Lee dead there'll be nobody to yell."

"You think she won't scream her head off?"

"Not when I get through with her she won't yell." Zack seemed pleased with the idea. "By the time they wake up in town to what's goin' on, there won't be enough beef left on Tres Pinos to stir dust."

Their horses climbed a long slope spotted by huisache and sotol. The day grew warmer. A buck deer broke from a thicket and went pounding over a ridge, dislodging some stones.

At the ridge, the three men drew rein to let their horses blow.

Lance rolled a cigarette, his yellow-flecked eyes thoughtful. "One thing you ain't thought of, Zack."

"What's that?"

"Just how you going to explain Boomer getting killed?"

"Simple. Boomer tried to arrest Rush for killin' Vic Peden. Rush shot Boomer. Hell, we three saw it. But Rush had a gun on us and we couldn't do nothing."

"When we caught Peden with his ear at the window," Lance grumbled, "you should have given your friend Rush the

212

same treatment. We'd have saved ourselves a lot of sweat."

"Don't call Rush no friend of mine." Zack turned on the black-haired Bagley, who was astride a lathered pinto. "I still can't see why the damn plan didn't work in town last night. With you and Lon both there."

"Rush was just too fast. He got Lon. And then a crowd came and I had to clear out!"

Zack's thick lips curled. "So damn simple and you two had to go and jam up the machinery."

"Wasn't our fault," Bagley said darkly.

"Hell, it would have worked. Lee fires Rush right in front of everybody. And to have Rush chase him outside and start yelling was perfect. And then Lee gets killed and the whole town blames Rush." Zack swore. "And even then with Lon on the roof and you at the corner, by God, you still couldn't make it work."

"I tell you there wasn't time. Rush must've seen Lon lookin' over the roof edge. Next thing I knowed, Lon was

213

down. And Lee was bleedin' like he'd been stuck with a butcher knife."

"Killin' Boomer this morning wasn't no improvement over the rest of your stupid mistake," Zack complained.

"With him ready to shoot my guts out? I'm s'posed to just stand there, huh?"

Zack started to make a further complaint, but Lance made an angry gesture. "Leave him alone, for kee-ryst sake. It's going to be our necks if we don't settle this thing."

"You don't have to remind me," was Zack's angry reply.

"Speaking of stupid mistakes," Lance said, turning in the saddle. "You had all the loose horses taken away from the home place and driven to roundup camp. We could use fresh mounts. Specially Clyde here."

Zack was staring at the sky. "I got a feelin' my luck is ridin' high. And when it does, not one damn thing goes wrong. We'll find Rush and the Magees."

When they reached Tres Pinos headquarters and scouted for sign, it was apparent that their quarry was heading north in a wagon.

Lance gave a shake of his dark head. "A wagon. When your luck's good, it's damned good, Zack."

Zack gave the other two a fierce smile. "They'll never outrun us in that wagon."

Bagley fingered scar tissue at a corner of his eye. "I owe that Rush Vining. I owe him so much he's goin' to bleed for it!"

"You'll have him," Zack predicted. "Before they even get within smellin' distance of the county seat."

17

WORRIEDLY Rush scanned their back trail. Not a half hour before he had seen dust, but then it had veered to the east. He hoped that whoever had stirred the dust was heading in the direction of Pilot Gap and would not swing north again.

He kept the team at a steady trot, angling toward the nearest water at Lobo Creek, a shallow stream that flowed between waist high banks of sand and screened by mesquite and juniper. Because of the heat the team needed water.

At the east bank of the creek he pulled up the team. "Eloise, you go down to the creek and unstrap that shotgun."

"It *is* uncomfortable," she admitted.

Rush tied the team to a deadfall and then swung her out of the wagon. "Another thing I realized," he smiled.

"You cracked me a good rap on the kneecap when I helped you into the wagon. I knew you didn't have a shin hard as gunmetal."

"I should have told you," she said. "But I—well, I just never wanted to go unarmed again."

"You still didn't trust me?"

"I do now, Rush." Her blue eyes looked up into his face. "Completely."

Lee, standing beside the wagon, looked fearfully back the way they had come. "God, can we reach Wheeler without something else happening?"

"Pray that we will," Rush said. "You'd better go with Eloise and give her a hand."

But Eloise said quickly, "I can manage." She was hobbling down a sandy path through towering mesquites, using the branches as handholds.

"Soon as she gets back," Rush said, "we'll fill our hats at the creek and let the horses drink." Then Rush made sure that the borrowed TT horse was still securely tied to the tailgate.

"I tell you one thing, Rush," Lee said, trying to roll a cigarette. His hands shook so he gave up. Rush rolled one for him as Lee continued, "Once Zack is disposed of, I'll feel reasonably safe with you running Tres Pinos."

A faint sound reached Rush. He tensed, peering toward the creek. But he could see nothing because of the towering growth. Probably Eloise getting rid of the shotgun, he decided.

Lee lit the cigarette Rush had rolled for him. "I think Eloise and I will travel for a time. Eventually we will settle back east, of course."

"I suppose that's best." Rush watched the ears of the team; Eloise seemed to be taking a long time for a simple chore of untying a shotgun.

"I know being in Texas has been an ordeal for me," Lee said. "Probably also an ordeal for Eloise."

"I would say so."

"But my stay here has done me some good. I remember Zack saying that people in town considered me a weakling.

Perhaps I was, at least in their eyes. In yours, Rush?"

Rush shrugged and peered toward the creek. "A lot of us are weak," he said.

"But I've gained considerable strength. I think now that it would be rather difficult to throw me off balance."

Rush noticed that a breeze, blowing from the south, suddenly shifted. And at that moment he heard a horse whinny from the direction of the far bank of the creek. At the same moment the ears of the wagon team shot forward.

"Come on," Rush snapped. "We'll take a look." Rush started toward a spot where mesquites were thinned out. A woman's scream ripped at his nerves.

He started to run. Ahead he could see the creek flowing between sand banks.

Directly ahead, on the far bank, Eloise sagged, her lower body in the creek. At her side, under the flowing water was the shotgun; even as Rush stared, some of the lashings she had used to fasten the weapon to her leg were floating away.

Brown fingers gripped her long golden

hair. His gaze shifted and he saw the sinewy arm attached to the sweat-gleaming torso of a Comanche. A young one. The brave stood with his body arched, his weight on the golden hair. He had pulled Eloise out of the creek where she had evidently fallen.

At that moment he saw Rush. Behind him on the brushy bank were two other braves astride cowponies, with four loose horses they had obviously stolen. Their glittering eyes were on Rush, their rifles lifting.

In that split second of time Rush made his decision.

The brave near Eloise would have to release her hair, then use the freed hand to line his rifle. Rush chose the first one on his left, fired, and the Comanche was slammed backward over the rump of his horse. The one on the right wheeled his pony, charged and Rush fired, missed.

A man's scream from behind Rush made the skin crawl. It was Lee, running. Not toward the Comanches, but away.

The brave on Rush's right jumped the

creek with his horse, caught up to Lee and swung the heavy butt of his rifle at Lee's head. Rush's shot caught the brave in the side. He fell hard, took a few staggering steps then collapsed. Lee continued running.

Rush swung back as a shot cut across the front of his shirt. Then the brave with Eloise, who had fired, dropped his rifle. He now held the point of a long-bladed knife against her throat. Her eyes were large, mirroring terror.

The brave wanted her alive; probably for later ransom. It was his mistake to misjudge Rush's cold nerve. Rush gambled and shot him in the face. Shot again and again, yelling at Eloise to twist aside. So that even an involuntary reflex could not trigger a bicep muscle that could plunge the knife into her throat.

As the Comanche shuddered and died, his blood darkening the creek, Rush picked her up. He stood with her, his rifle cocked, ready to fire one-handed into her skull if more Comanches swarmed on them and there was no way to prevent her capture. But none appeared. Horses of the dead braves and the loose ones were running away. The sounds of their flight continued for some time.

Eloise locked her fingers around Rush's neck, and her full trembling weight sagged against him. "I had just freed the shotgun," she breathed against Rush's chest. "The next thing I knew he had me by the hair."

"We had luck. There were only three of them. And they concentrated on you."

"Because I am a woman," she said and shuddered.

"Not just any woman. Yellow hair is highly prized."

"Rush, without you I would be dead."

"No. But in time you might have prayed for it."

Then she said, "I heard a terrible sound. Was it Lee?"

"Yes."

"Is he alive?"

"The last I saw of him he was."

"He ran, didn't he?" She tilted her face

against his chest, her large eyes searching his face.

"Lee should have suffered through his youth and stayed in Texas. It might have toughened him. Living with an aunt—well, some men it weakens. I've said too much."

She unlocked her fingers. "I can stand alone now. My knees were so weak."

"No wonder."

She shaded her eyes to stare across the rolling rangeland. "Where is he?"

Rush shrugged. "I won't leave you here alone. So we'll go after him together."

But they didn't have to hunt Lee. He came walking along the road, sweated, his hair disheveled. In his wild flight he had evidently stumbled. His face was scratched, the shirt torn. Lee slowed to look at the crumpled brave who had tried to brain him.

"He's dead," Lee said. Then he crossed to where Rush and Eloise were standing. "I'm sorry I ran." Lee was breathing hard. "I guess I panicked. Eloise, are you all right?"

She started to answer, then she looked away and climbed into the wagon.

"Keep your eye on her," Rush snapped, then retraced his steps to the creek to inspect the bodies of the other two Comanches. The one who had dragged Eloise by her hair had no face. The other one was also quite dead. Straining his ears, Rush listened for any sounds that would indicate more Comanches in the area. But all he heard was the ripple of the creek over flat stones. He could see the blood on the sand, the horse droppings, the indentation made by Eloise's body. How close it had been. Cold sweat broke out on his back.

The Comanches had come from the west, according to the tracks he could see in the sand, their only object to water their horses and push on. But they had spotted Eloise and been so fascinated by the sight of the golden-haired one they had not been prepared for a shift in the breeze that betrayed their presence.

When Rush got back to the wagon he

saw Lee, his scratched face without color so that the marks were livid. Mechanically, Lee brushed at twigs that clung to his clothing. Rush untied the team.

"Why didn't you say something?" Lee cried. "Is it the crime of the century because I ran?"

"Lee, get in the wagon," Eloise said.

Lee's mouth shook. He started to say something, then got in beside her.

Rush gathered in the lines. "We'd better put some miles between us and this place. No telling who might have heard the shooting. Sound travels far."

Lee was hunched in the seat, hands gripping his kneecaps. "I just panicked. My whole body seemed to go to pieces inside. All I thought about was saving my life."

They drove for a mile, two miles.

Finally Lee cried, "Say something! For kee-ryst sake, call me a coward!"

"It doesn't matter now," Eloise said.

"Why don't you accuse me of running, Rush? At a time when my wife was being dragged by a renegade. Who later would probably have raped her. Maybe even killed her—" Lee's voice broke. "I suppose you're through with me." He glanced at Eloise, as if fearful of what she might say.

The rumbling wheels of the wagon made several revolutions before Eloise spoke. "We'll go east. This country isn't for you."

"Nor for you."

"At one time it wasn't."

Lee looked at her in surprise. "You mean you could live in this hellish place? Eloise, you must be mad."

"Lee, will you kindly shut up." Eloise's voice was ragged.

As they topped a rise, Rush saw a plume of dust. The wind that had alerted him to the presence of the Comanches at the creek had also flatted out the column of dust until now—the dust moving toward them from the north. Down in a shallow valley Rush could see three dots moving across the brushy flats. Hopefully, Rush watched the trio for a moment, thinking they were going to bypass them. Then Rush knew the wagon had been spotted. Their own dust was towering behind them.

Lee had also seen the distant riders. "Oh, God, what now?"

"I've got a hunch it's Zack," Rush said, his mouth suddenly dry. "They circled around and came in ahead of us."

Eloise made a small sound of despair. "I forgot the shotgun. It fell in the creek."

"No use to us anyway. Not until we could dry it out."

"What will we do, Rush?" she asked anxiously.

"If you could only ride a horse."

"I can try," she said quickly.

"This is no time for riding lessons." He began to look for a place where they could make a stand.

18

NOW the three horsemen were nearer, but they would have to climb a long brushy slope in order to reach this tableland Rush was now crossing with the wagon. No matter how he figured it, the odds were three to one. Eloise was certainly inexperienced when it came to firearms. And Lee could not be counted upon at all. He might panic again as he had when the Comanches tried to abduct Eloise.

The nearest shelter was some rocks, waist high, some fifty yards to his right. By keeping down, the granite barrier would offer some protection. But for how long? This unanswered question turned him cold.

"We'll have to make a stand," he announced and turned the team and his tied-on saddler toward the ring of rocks.

"I think we should try and outrun them," Lee said nervously.

Rush didn't even bother to reply. He drove the team far back in the rocks and tied them. Then he handed Lee one of the rifles and some shells. The third rifle he gave to Eloise.

"Can you shoot one of these?" Rush asked.

"I'll watch how you do it, Rush."

He nodded and gave her a tight smile. "Afraid?"

She turned her large eyes on him. "Never again in my life will I be as frightened as I was there on that creek bank."

Lee watched them narrowly for a moment. Then he said, "I suppose the decent thing would be to let Eloise get a divorce."

"Lee, will you please be quiet?" Eloise turned on him.

"A divorce isn't so uncommon. I recall a friend of Aunt Lottie's who divorced her husband. Of course there was scandal, but—"

Rush hit him on the shoulder with the

flat of his hand. "Fire that rifle when I tell you. In the meantime stop making things harder for Eloise."

Rush turned his attention to the lip of the tableland some eighty yards away. Now he could hear their horses climbing up the slant. Then there would be open country for them to cross, until they reached the crown of the hill where Rush had decided to make his stand. To his right was the only cover, a rise of ground covered thickly with junipers not quite half the distance to the drop off where Zack would likely appear at any moment. The click of shod hooves on rock became louder. A horse whinnied.

"Can we fight them off?" Eloise asked tensely.

"Unless Zack gets into those junipers without us seeing him. He could pick us off."

"It doesn't look very promising," she said, and tried to smile.

The three of them had been kneeling behind the rocks, peering over the tops. Suddenly Lee stood up.

Rush could not hide his irritation. "Get down. Do you want your head shot off?"

Instead of answering, Lee vaulted the barrier of rock, rifle in hand. He started trotting toward the riders who now had appeared over the lip of the table, Zack and Oro Lance.

Lee twisted around, looking back at Rush and Eloise. "I'll settle your problems for you, Eloise!" Lee shouted. "Settle them once and for all!"

Rush cried, "Lee. Come back! Don't act like a damn fool!"

But Lee kept going directly toward Zack and Lance. Rush fired, trying to drop Lance, who was slightly ahead of Zack. But the shot went wide as Lance spurred in, shouting something. A rope snaked out of the junipers to Lee's right. A noose settled over Lee's head.

Zack's booming voice reached Rush and the girl.

"Step down here, you two! You got one half minute. Or I'll send you Lee's head in a sack!"

"How horrible!" Eloise shuddered.

Rush saw Lee jerked off his feet by the roper who was back in the junipers. Lee lost his grip on the rifle. Each time he tried to get up, he was pulled down again. With Lee clutching at the rope to take the strain off his neck, the roper pulled him into the junipers.

Rush licked dry lips. "What happens to Mrs. Magee if I give myself up?" Rush shouted.

"She'll live!" Zack, sitting in his saddle, seemed almost jaunty about it. He presented a broad target, as if confident Rush would hold his fire as long as Lee was a prisoner.

Eloise reached out and gripped Rush by the wrist. "You're not to give yourself up," she said fiercely.

"I'll do it to save your life."

"I'm still a woman, don't forget. And will I receive any better treatment at the hands of Zack than I would have with that renegade you killed?"

"Not much to choose, I agree." Rush kept his eyes locked on the pair down the gentle slope.

And then Bagley rode out of the junipers, hauling Lee by the rope. Lee moved at a stumbling walk. He fell, picked himself up. What a pathetic figure he made, Rush had to admit.

"Poor Lee," Eloise sobbed. "Why did he try to be a hero?"

The three riders dismounted. Zack caught Lee by the front of the torn shirt, said something to him. Then he backhanded Lee across the face. Lee's knees buckled. But Zack pulled him up and in close against his broad chest.

"Rush, you better get down here. Or Mrs. Magee won't have a husband!" Zack shouted at them.

Eloise's eyes were frantic. "What can we do?"

Keeping down, Rush transferred his belt gun to his waistband. He pulled his shirt down to hide the gun. "All I can do is hope to get in close enough to get in a shot."

"Once you step out there they'll kill you. Rush don't—"

She reached for his arm, trying to hold

him. But he had already made up his mind.

Suddenly Lee came to life. He did a surprising thing. Never would Rush forget that moment if he lived to be a hundred. Lee righted himself and pressed closer to Zack as if to embrace the big man. Lee's two arms went around Zack's waist, pinning the arms. Lee's fingers locked together at Zack Henley's back.

"Rush!" Lee cried. "Your chance!" He screamed it, not in hysteria. It was not the terrible sound he had made when the Comanches struck. This scream was almost a battle cry.

Bagley was the first to fire up at the circle of rocks. The bullet scream away. Rush answered the shot with one of his own. Bagley's right shoulder collapsed, he spun, went down and made a few awkward scrabbling motions in the grass.

Lance took one look at Zack, big, red-faced now, whirling Lee around and around in his wild attempt to break loose the locked arms that pinned him.

It all happened so quickly that Rush

was just levering another shell into his rifle after shooting Bagley when Lance moved. Lance's hand flashed for the deadly gun at his belt, drew it and fired once into Lee's body. Lee slumped, cried out, but still kept his hold on Zack's midsection. Lance was coming toward the circle of rocks at a crouching, zig-zag run. The black hat was pulled low, the gold piece on the chin strap bouncing across the front of his shirt.

Bullets from Lance's gun ricocheted into the rock circle and Rush was forced to take his eyes of the target in order to push Eloise down, out of comparative danger.

When he straightened up he saw that twenty yards separated Lance from the ring of rocks. Lance was coming at a run. Just as Rush fired his rifle, something with the impact of a runaway horse knocked him down. Dazedly he came to his knees, the rifle lying a yard away. Reaching out, he snatched up the hot weapon and fired it. But Lance still advanced. Again Rush fired as a bullet cut across his right side. A cry of dismay

235

burst from Rush as he tried to hang onto his swimming senses; Lance was still coming. The white teeth gleamed, but the head was tipped forward. Lance lost his balance, fell to his knees. He tried to lift his gun, but it fell out of his hand. He fell over on his side.

Downslope, Lee had been flung aside by Zack. In his rage at Lee, Zack's murderous temper was the end of his luck. He turned his gun on Lee and fired shot after shot into his body. Because Lee had spoiled it all for him. So typical of Zack.

Rush managed to press his left hip against a rock in order to steady his shaking body. But big Zack presented a fuzzy target. It took two shots before Rush saw Zack reel aside.

Zack shouted something that sounded like, "Hell of a friend you turned out to be—"

Rush's third shot drilled squarely into the center of Zack's broad face. . . .

No one in Pilot Gap ever forgot the day

that the eastern girl, Lee Magee's widow, drove a spring wagon into Lake's wagonyard, her hair wild, her dress torn, wearing only one shoe.

Beside her, hunched over in the seat, nearly unconscious from loss of blood, Rush Vining clung to the back of the seat. In the bed of the wagon was the body of Lee Magee, and beside it, trussed up despite a broken shoulder, was Clyde Bagley.

Only when Rush was certain that Eloise was safely in town did he completely let go.

For a week the rooms at the wagonyard looked like a hospital. Finally came a day when Rush found that he had an appetite.

Later that day he and Eloise talked about Lee and the rest of it. Sheriff Faulkner had come down from the county seat to take Bagley into custody. Bagley, a man in pain and fearing death, had told all.

The sheriff looked in on Rush, saying, "Now that you're the surviving partner in Tres Pinos, aside from the widow, that is,

I just want you to know there's no hard feelings. I never cared much for that shirttail kin you shot anyhow."

"I understand," Rush said, and would have laughed had not the days been so tragic.

"Anything you need down this way, just let me know." Sheriff Faulkner cleared his throat. "Just before he died— got murdered," the sheriff amended, "Charlie wrote a note to his lawyer Flannery. Must've done it sometime that Saturday night. He slipped it under Flannery's office door. Flannery found it when he got back from Austin this morning. Charlie wanted you to have Zack's fifteen per cent. Reckon Zack was the cow thief, not you, and Charlie was fixin' to fire him."

When the sheriff had departed Rush stirred in his blankets. "From segundo to part owner. Makes a difference in how a man's treated. I guess Faulkner hasn't forgotten that it's the cowmen who elect sheriffs in this country."

Eloise, sitting beside the bed, said, "What do we do now, Rush?"

"I suppose you'll want to go east and —and get over Lee."

"Not necessarily. I'm sorry for Lee. But the feeling was gone. Long before I came with him to Texas."

"Too bad that tradition says a widow has to wait a full year before remarrying."

"I broke tradition once in this town. I wore a yellow dress to Charlie Magee's funeral."

"I don't think he would have minded at all."

"And would he mind the other—us?"

"A lot of people made Lee what he was. I think Charlie was mostly to blame. Lee did a senseless heroic thing. But it probably saved our lives . . . no, I don't think Charlie would mind."

"I'd like to be married in that yellow dress. It symbolizes a passing. And also a beginning."

FARGO: MASSACRE RIVER
by John Benteen

Fargo spurred his horse to the edge of the road. The ambushers up ahead had now blocked the road. Fargo's convoy was a jumble, a perfect target for the insurgents' weapons!

SUNDANCE: DEATH IN THE LAVA
by John Benteen

The land echoed with the thundering hoofs of Modoc ponies. In minutes they swooped down and captured the wagon train and its cargo of gold. But now the halfbreed they called Sundance was going after it, and he swore nothing would stand in his way.

GUNS OF FURY
by Ernest Haycox

Dane Starr, alias Dan Smith, wanted to close the door on his past and hang up his guns, but people wouldn't let him. Good men wanted him to settle their scores for them. Bad men thought they were faster and itched to prove it. Starr had to keep killing just to stay alive.

FARGO: PANAMA GOLD
by John Benteen

Cleve Buckner was recruiting an army of killers, gunmen and deserters from all over Central America. With foreign money behind him, Buckner was going to destroy the Panama Canal before it could be completed. Fargo's job was to stop Buckner—and to eliminate him once and for all!

FARGO: THE SHARPSHOOTERS
by John Benteen

The Canfield clan, thirty strong, were raising hell in Texas. One of them had shot a Texas Ranger, and the Rangers had to bring in the killer. Fargo was tough enough to hold his own against the whole clan.

SUNDANCE: OVERKILL
by John Benteen

Sundance's reputation as a fighting man had spread. There was no job too tough for the halfbreed to handle. So when a wealthy banker's daughter was kidnapped by the Cheyenne, he offered Sundance $10,000 to rescue the girl.

HELL RIDERS
by Steve Mensing

Wade Walker's kid brother, Duane, was locked up in the Silver City jail facing a rope at dawn. Wade was a ruthless outlaw, but he was smart, and he had vowed to have his brother out of jail before morning!

DESERT OF THE DAMNED
by Nelson Nye

The law was after him for the murder of a marshal—a murder he didn't commit. Breen was after him for revenge—and Breen wouldn't stop at anything . . . blackmail, a frameup . . . or murder.

DAY OF THE COMANCHEROS
by Steven C. Lawrence

Their very name struck terror into men's hearts—the Comancheros, a savage army of cutthroats who swept across Texas, leaving behind a bloodstained trail of robbery and murder.

SUNDANCE: SILENT ENEMY
by John Benteen

Both the Indians and the U.S. Cavalry were being victimized. A lone crazed Cheyenne was on a personal war path against both sides. They needed to pit one man against one crazed Indian. That man was Sundance.

LASSITER
by Jack Slade

Lassiter wasn't the kind of man to listen to reason. Cross him once and he'd hold a grudge for years to come—if he let you live that long. But he was no crueler than the men he had killed, and he had never killed a man who didn't need killing.

LAST STAGE TO GOMORRAH
by Barry Cord

Jeff Carter, tough ex-riverboat gambler, now had himself a horse ranch that kept him free from gunfights and card games. Until Sturvesant of Wells Fargo showed up. Jeff owed him a favour and Sturvesant wanted it paid up. All he had to do was to go to Gomorrah and recover a quarter of a million dollars stolen from a stagecoach!

McALLISTER ON THE COMANCHE CROSSING
by Matt Chisholm

The Comanche, deadly warriors and the finest horsemen in the world, reckon McAllister owes them a life—and the trail is soaked with the blood of the men who had tried to outrun them before.

QUICK-TRIGGER COUNTRY
by Clem Colt

Turkey Red hooked up with Curly Bill Graham's outlaw crew and soon made a name for himself. But wholesale murder was out of Turk's line, so when range war flared he bucked the whole border gang alone . . .

PISTOL LAW
by Paul Evan Lehman

Lance Jones came back to Mustang for just one thing—Revenge! Revenge on the people who had him thrown in jail; on the crooked marshal; on the human vulture who had already taken over the town. Now it was Lance's turn . . .

GUNSLINGER'S RANGE
by Jackson Cole

Three escaped convicts are out for revenge. They won't rest until they put a bullet through the head of the dirty snake who locked them behind bars.

RUSTLER'S TRAIL
by Lee Floren

Jim Carlin knew he would have to stand up and fight because he had staked his claim right in the middle of Big Ike Outland's best grass. Jim also had a score to settle with his renegade brother.

Larry and Stretch:
THE TRUTH ABOUT SNAKE RIDGE
by Marshall Grover

The troubleshooters came to San Cristobal to help the needy. For Larry and Stretch the turmoil began with a brawl, then an ambush, and then another attempt on their lives—all in one day.

WOLF DOG RANGE
by Lee Floren

Montana was big country, but not big enough for a ruthless land-grabber like Will Ardery. He would stop at nothing, unless something stopped him first—like a bullet from Pete Manly's gun.

Larry and Stretch: DEVIL'S DINERO
by Marshall Grover

Plagued by remorse, a rich old reprobate hired the Texas Troubleshooters to deliver a fortune in greenbacks to each of his victims. Even before Larry and Stretch rode out of Cheyenne, a traitor was selling the secret and the hunt was on.

CAMPAIGNING
by Jim Miller

Ambushed on the Santa Fe trail, Sean Callahan is saved from dying by two Indian strangers. Then the trio is joined by a former slave called Hannibal. But there'll be more lead and arrows flying before the band join the legendary Kit Carson in his campaign against the Comanches.

DONOVAN
by Elmer Kelton

Donovan was supposed to be dead. The town had buried him years before when Uncle Joe Vickers had fired off both barrels of a shotgun into the vicious outlaw's face as he was escaping from jail. Now Uncle Joe had been shot—in just the same way.

CODE OF THE GUN
by Gordon D. Shirreffs

MacLean came riding home with saddle-tramp written all over him, but sewn in his shirt-lining was an Arizona Ranger's star. MacLean had his own personal score to settle—in blood and violence!

GAMBLER'S GUN LUCK
by Brett Austen

Gamblers hands are clean and quick with cards, guns and women. But their names are black, and they seldom live long. Parker was a hell of a gambler. It was his life—or his death . . .